Strange Fruit Stories

Strange Fruit Stories

The untold in one setting

Volume One

Tina E. Pope

iUniverse LLC
Bloomington

STRANGE FRUIT STORIES
The Untold in One Setting, Volume One

iUniverse books may be ordered through booksellers or by contacting:

iUniverse LLC
1663 Liberty Drive
Bloomington, IN 47403
www.iuniverse.com
1-800-Authors (1-800-288-4677)

ISBN: 978-1-4502-9956-5 (sc)
ISBN: 978-1-4502-9957-2 (e)

Printed in the United States of America.

iUniverse rev. date: 11/11/2013

Chapter One

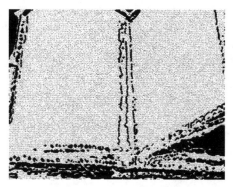

The thief comes only in order to steal and kill and destroy;
I have come that they may have and enjoy life, and have it to the full.

—John 10:10 (NKJV)

Hello, my name is Joanna Miller, but people around here call me Joe. I'm a young girl. I lived in a town called Oak Steel, where people disappeared. If people questioned or even seemed like they were seeking the truth, they were killed—like Ms. Annabelle. She was the owner of one of the best tailor shops in town. She was very outspoken, willing to help others, and stood by what she believed in. Ms. Annabelle would always give this speech.

"Death around here is like a common cold; sooner or later, it will end up at your door. There's nowhere you can go to get a peace of mind; that's where Satan is trying his best to control your mind. This world and the things in it are designed to poison your secret thoughts. Responding to the wrong voices may cost you your soul. With God's help, that's the only way you can transform your mind. Don't be a fool; you can't do it on your own. Before you know it, hell has become your home and you're on your knees praying, crying, screaming, and wishing you would have chosen the narrow road. What my very own eyes have seen, my heart doesn't agree with, but I know there's more to it than what they wanted me to believe. If God doesn't exist, why must they fight against what I believe? Who am I hurting by wanting to love and to help those who are in need?

"Oak Steel has built a case against me, but their evidence is weak. The town is known for gathering false information, twisting words, accusing people, and killing the innocent just to put fear into those who are weak. By their actions, it is very clear to see they are afraid of the truth. They are determined to keep the book hidden because of the secret treasures that will be revealed—knowing the secret's treasures and receiving the promises of God that are given only to his children who believe. If we had this knowledge, it would make their position in this world weak. So they must convince us that God is not real and kill those who do believe."

After every speech, I would clap my hands. Ms. Annabelle spoke with so much authority, and her words made me think. Even though I was puzzled by the things she said, somehow, I knew her words were true.

I met Ms. Annabelle about two years ago when my stepfather, Steve, and I went to pick up some clothing that he had dropped off at her store earlier in the week. When we walked in, Ms. Annabelle was sitting down reading a book. Her husband took care of my father. Steve was so upset with Ms. Annabelle that he started screaming and yelling at her husband.

"Daddy, calm down. What is wrong?" I asked him. I had never seen Steve act this way before. My stepfather was acting like a fool. Mr. Liam never lost his cool, and Ms. Annabelle never looked up. Their reaction to his behavior made him very upset.

He snatched the clothing out of Mr. Liam's hands, and then he turned to me and said, "I never want you to come in here, do you hear me?"

"Yes," I said, but I couldn't figure out why he was so mad at Ms. Annabelle. Him commanding me not to go back into the store made me want to even more.

I would sneak behind my parents' backs and go see Ms. Annabelle every day before and after school to get help with my reading. In this town, they set a limit on how far a girl could go with her education. I personally wanted more out of life. The women here could barely read and were forced to marry men they did not know. Some of the families around here made money by selling their daughters. I was next in line and worried about what type of man I would have as my husband. There were many who watched me and approached with sex in their eyes. So I carried a rock just in case I had to hit a few. I didn't want them touching me; some of these men could be my grandfather. It wouldn't matter how much I resisted, whoever had the most money would get me. The closer it came to the time for me to be married off, the more my mother began to talk to me about what to expect on that night of being with a man. I hated those talks, and I never paid attention to what she had to say. She would yell and scream and then ask me what I wanted to do with my life. "I want to go to school and make something of myself," I would tell her time after time. In return, I was told an educated woman wouldn't do well around there and that was why they could never know about Ms. Annabelle.

My reading began to improve after two months. She taught me how to type and sew. I began to learn a lot from Ms. Annabelle. I could see why the people in town didn't like her. She knew more and had more than some of the men in Oak Steel, and the town was not open to change.

Knowing what she knew and living the life that she lived, Ms. Annabelle would be able to change the minds of others and that became a problem for some of the folks in town—a major problem that would end up getting Mr. Liam murdered. He was found dead in his car, shot three times in the head. Ms. Annabelle was the one who found him. After Mr. Liam's death, there was talk around town, but she never worried about the things that were being said or the threats that were made against her life. Knowing you're about to die would normally cause a person to worry. Not Ms. Annabelle. For some reason, I felt she knew her time had come because of the things she would say to me.

I went to check on Ms. Annabelle one day after school just to see how she was coping with her husband's death. When she opened the door, I could tell by her eyes that she had been crying. I couldn't stand seeing her like this. I wished there was something I could do to take away her pain. As Ms. Annabelle closed the door behind me, she asked what I was doing there.

"This place is no longer safe for you," she said to me.

"I know, but I needed to see you."

"You shouldn't have come."

"But I was worried about you."

"Worried about me? Why, Joe?"

"I thought you would be worried about what they might do to you now that your husband is dead," I said to her.

Ms. Annabelle turned to me and said, "I'm not worried, Joe, and you shouldn't be either. You have been around my husband and me too long, and you have seen so much. That's why I don't understand why you would be worried. Mr. Liam and I both knew what we signed up for, and I don't regret it, not one bit."

We both just stood there in silence. Since I had nothing else to say, I began to help her pack the rest of Mr. Liam's things.

Mr. Liam believed that a woman should have the same rights as a man. He had no problems with his wife being able to read and with her working. Mr. Liam would always say, "It's always better to have a wife who is able to work with you than to have a wife who can never make a decision without you." Now that Mr. Liam was dead, we all knew she would be next. Ms. Annabelle went on living her life as she would have if Mr. Liam were still alive.

As I was folding a pair of Mr. Liam's pants, Ms. Annabelle said to me, "Joe, you fear no man. If you fear man, the kingdom inside of you will fall."

The kingdom inside of you? What is she talking about? I didn't quite understand what she meant, but every time I was in her shop, I felt good. She would tell me things and show me things that no one else ever had. Seeing how loving Ms. Annabelle was, it made me want to be just like her. Sometimes, I wished I was her daughter, so I wouldn't have to go home. I hated going home. I had my reasons for not wanting to walk through that door. My home wasn't peaceful. Depression and anger had taken over the atmosphere.

One night, I was awakened by screams coming from downstairs. When I reached the top step, I saw my stepfather holding the shotgun in one hand and my brother in the other. My mother was on her knees, crying and begging him not to shoot James. By the look on James's face, I could tell he was scared. "Please!" I screamed. "Let him go! Mother, help! Don't let him do this again!"

My little sisters came out from their bedroom. "What's going on, Joe?" one of them asked me.

"Go back in the room, lock the door, and don't come out!" I ordered them. They ran back into their room and locked the door. I looked back downstairs and saw my stepfather had the gun pressed against my brother's head.

I heard a voice say, "He's going to kill him."

"No!" I yelled as I was running down the steps. It was too late. *No, it can't be. I can't believe it! My brother is dead.* James's body lay there covered with blood. I bent down and held his head in my arms.

"What did I do?" my stepfather kept saying as he walked back and forth. "How did this gun get in my hand?"

My mother was trying to touch James, but I wouldn't let her. "Get away!" I yelled at her. *Why did she move this man into our home? She barely knew him. Allowing him to hurt us, punishment after punishment and being beaten for no reason.* The only things I could say to her at that moment were the words, "I hate you."

Steve walked over to Mother and said, "We have to get rid of the body."

She looked at me and then said, "I'm sorry, Joe. I needed him," and then she tried to touch James again.

"What? Do not touch him," I said to them.

"Get up," he said to me.

I stood up covered with James's blood and watched them drag his body out the back door. I went to my bedroom and locked the door. I could hear my little sisters crying. I changed my clothes and then went inside their room.

"What happened? What was all that noise?" they asked me.

"Don't worry. Everything will be okay," I said to them.

"Where is James?" they asked.

Before I could answer, my mother walked in. "You girls go sleep in my bed tonight," she said to them.

"Joe?" they both said.

I wanted them to stay, but I knew it was best for them to leave. "Go," I said to them.

My mother walked over and said, "Joe, I'm so sorry. I don't know what to do," and then she tried to touch me.

"Don't," I said to her.

"This is not my fault. You blame me?" she asked.

"Yes, you are the one to blame."

"I'm afraid of what he might do to you. Why can't you just behave? Then Steve wouldn't be so angry," she said to me.

"We are the ones to blame, Mother? What did James do? Huh? Tell me? What have I ever done?" I said to her.

"You bastards were born. I have the right to be happy. No good man wanted me, because I had too many kids, and when Steve came along, he took care of us and paid the bills!" she yelled at me.

"You have one thing right, Mother; he took, but he took things that didn't belong to him."

"Do you want to die? Wind up like your brother?" she asked me.

"I want to go to Grandma's house. Send me there," I said to her.

"My mother's? You think she will treat you better? Where do you think this sickness came from?" she said to me as she walked out the door.

I went back to my room and sat in the chair until daybreak.

As soon as I saw a sign of light, I went straight to Ms. Annabelle's shop. I had to get out of the house. She wondered why I was there so early, but I didn't want to tell her the things that were going on at home. Ms. Annabelle walked over and put her arms around me, and then I began to cry. It was a relief to release the anger and pain that I held inside. She wiped my face and told me that she loved me.

"You love me? Why?" I asked.

"Because of who you are," she answered.

"Who am I?"

"A child, a child of God," Ms. Annabelle said to me.

"No, you're wrong. I'm a child of a woman who beats me, curses me out, and always talks down to me. My father, my real father, moved on and married another woman and forgot about me. This stepfather of mine is a monster in a dream that I can't wake up from."

"You're hurting right now, and that's okay, but one day, you will understand it all," she said and then walked away. I followed.

She sat in her chair and reached for a book that was on the table.

"What are you reading? Is that the same book that I see you reading all the time?" I asked.

"Yes, it is."

"I tried to read it but could not understand what I was reading. Can you read it to me?"

"I will, but you have to pay attention."

I told her that I would and sat patiently as she read.

After Ms. Annabelle read some of the book to me, my curiosity got the best of me, so I asked her a few questions. I wanted to know about this God who called himself I Am and claimed he is able to do all things. He also stated he is a powerful, truthful God and he would never leave or forsake us. Could this be true? If so, where is he? And where did he come from? I had never heard of any person who would want to take on someone else's problems, but this God in heaven wanted to? "Why is that?" I asked her. As you can see, I had so many questions. She couldn't answer them all, because the door was kicked in. I jumped and moved closer to Ms. Annabelle.

She turned me around and staring me right in the face, said, "Go and hide. Take these books with you."

"What's going on?"

"Go now! Hide in the closet, and don't come out," she said in a low voice.

I grabbed the books and went to hide in the closet. The door was not shut all the way. A few seconds later, three men walked past the closet door. Ms. Annabelle never got out of the chair. She sat there with her hands folded. One of the men stood in front of her with his fist balled. He said something to her in a low voice before he hit her.

"Jesus, help me, please!" she called out loud.

"Where is it?" one of the men asked her, before striking her again in the face.

"Where is what?" she asked.

"You stupid fool!" He hit her twice in the face.

"You will never find it, and you will never keep it a secret," Ms. Annabelle said to them.

"Do you really think you can stop me?" he said to her.

"Oh, not me, but my father can," she said to them.

"Your father? Who is this man that you speak of?" he asked her.

"God, he calls himself I Am," she said to them.

"Is this the same God that your husband spoke about before we killed him?" he asked.

"Yes, he is the same God then and the same God now."

"This God is supposed to love you, but he will let you die. Is that love?" he asked her.

"My God is not like man; his ways are not your ways. Why my God does what he does, only he knows. My only purpose is to do his will, and it's done," she said.

"So you'd rather die for a God that you have never seen than live?" he asked her.

"I have seen my father; he's always here," she said to them.

"Where are you? Do you even care about what will happen to her? What kind of God are you that you allow people to be put to death just to honor your name?" he said out loud.

"Liam," she called out.

"What did you say?" he asked.

"It's time," Ms. Annabelle told them.

"Where is it?" he asked once again.

Ms. Annabelle stopped talking to them and began saying these words over and over again. "Yea, though I walk through the valley of the shadow of death, I will fear no evil; for You *are* with me; your rod and your staff, they comfort me . . ."

He grabbed the bottle from off the table and hit Ms. Annabelle across the head. Her body fell out of the chair and landed on the floor. I knew she was dead. I bit down on one of the books to stop myself from screaming. The next thing I knew, those men began ransacking the store. "Where are those damn books?" one of the men said out loud.

Could I have the books that they are looking for? Before I knew it, the closet door opened. I was standing right in front of him, but for some reason, he didn't see me. I stood still anyway and waited for them to leave, which they did. I walked over to her and touched her face. I couldn't believe she was dead. I heard footsteps approaching. I ran behind the chair. It was so huge and beautiful at the same time. The light coming from it hurt my eyes. It walked over to

Ms. Annabelle and stretched out a hand. Ms. Annabelle grabbed it and stood up, but her body was still lying on the floor. How could that be? Was I seeing two Ms. Annabelles at the same time? I stood there crying, not because I was scared, but because deep down inside, I wanted to go with her. Ms. Annabelle might be going to this place called heaven she had always spoken about. This heaven was better than being on earth, according to Ms. Annabelle. If so, I didn't want to be left behind.

"Ms. Annabelle!" I yelled. "Please don't leave me! I want to come with you!"

She turned around and said to me, "Joe, you can't come with me. God has a job for you."

"Is that God that you are with?" I asked her.

"No, Joe. It's an angel," she said as they disappeared.

I reached for the blanket that was on the chair and covered Ms. Annabelle's body with it and then ran out the back door.

What do I do now? I need someone to talk to, but who can I tell? Who would believe me? Speaking of such things would lead a person to being placed in a mental institution. If that happened, I would never learn the truth.

So I decided to take the long way home. I needed some time to think. Three people I had loved so dearly had left me. Now I had no choice but to go home. These books must be very important for them to kill for them. What are they trying to hide? I asked myself. I had about four more blocks before I reached home. When I began approaching the third block, the police stopped everyone and forced them into the middle of the street. I wanted to run the other way, but a woman grabbed me and said, "If you run, they will find you." I just looked at her, wondering who she was, but I did what she said and stood still. She gave me a bag to put the books in. I waited to hear the reason why the police had stopped us. We stood there waiting for the sheriff to arrive; a few minutes later, he did. The police car pulled up, and they threw a tall, skinny man out of the car. He fell to the ground, and we could tell that he had been beaten before they brought him there. His face and hands were covered with blood. His left eye was swollen shut. The man's clothing was filthy, and he had no shoes on his feet.

"Please believe I did not kill Ms. Annabelle!" he said.

One of the police officers walked over and kicked him. He said, "Didn't I tell you to shut up?"

That voice! That's one of the three men who was there when Ms. Annabelle died. The police are behind her death. Who sent them to do their dirty work? I looked up at the woman who was holding my arm. She looked down at me and put her finger over her lips. I turned my eyes back to the sheriff. I watched him walk back and forth in front of the crowd for a while before he began to speak.

"What's going on?" someone yelled from the crowd.

"This man right here is behind all the killing in this town. This morning, we caught him leaving Ms. Annabelle's store, and now she is dead," the sheriff told us.

The crowd looked at each other like they couldn't believe what they were hearing. Some knew the man who was being accused and were surprised by what they had heard.

The stranger stood up and said, "My name is Robert James. I did not kill her. She was dead when I walked in. Some of you know me very well. I would never commit murder. What would be the cause?" Those who knew him turned their heads.

"He's a liar; I have two witnesses who saw him kill Ms. Annabelle," the sheriff said.

"Where are they?" the man yelled out loud.

"This man and this woman saw him kill Ms. Annabelle," the sheriff said to the crowd as he pointed to the witnesses.

The stranger walked over to them and said, "Are you going to stand there and say you saw me kill Ms. Annabelle? I have a wife and a family; your lies will cause me to be put to death."

The man and woman stood there and didn't say a word. The sheriff pulled out his gun. Some of the people in the crowd turned their heads. I began to pull my arm free from the woman, but she was gone. I ran home in fear, not knowing what would happen to me.

I stayed quiet watching the killers go on with their daily lives, until one morning when I was awakened by a tapping sound. I sat up, and there he was, the young man I had watched being murdered, standing at the foot of my bed. I rubbed my eyes to make sure this was what I was actually seeing. Another man then stepped from behind him. I got up and sat in my chair in the corner. He walked over and sat on my bed. We were facing one another, and I wondered what to say.

"You can see me?" he asked.

"Yes," I answered.

"My name is Peter Long, and you are?" he asked.

"My name is Joe," I said to him.

"You know what happened to Ms. Annabelle?" he asked me.

"Yes, but I couldn't help her," I said to him.

"But you can help her now, Joe."

"No, I can't. If the word gets out that I know who killed her, they will kill me and my family. Those men are bad men; they are involved in some terrible things. They were asking about a book. Do you know anything about it?" I asked him.

He smiled at me and then said, "I do."

"Can you tell me what's going on? Do they know that I have the book?" I asked him.

"Not yet, but they will," he said to me. "That's why we have to go."

"Go where?" I asked him.

"You must hurry. Move now. Ask questions later," Peter urged me.

Before I could ask another question, others came to stand around him. Men, women, and children of all ages were gathered together, looking at me. Some had scars, bruises, burns, missing body parts, and gunshot wounds.

"Who are they?" I asked him with fear in my voice.

"Don't be scared, Joe," Peter said. "They won't hurt you, not these spirits."

"So why are they here?" I asked.

"They have their own stories to tell and want them to be known. There was an older woman who helped them for many years, but she's dead now."

"Are you talking about Ms. Annabelle? She was trying to explain to me about some God," I said.

"Some God, you say, Joe? You just don't know."

I kept quiet to allow him to finish speaking.

"Ms. Annabelle is not the woman I am speaking of, but she was part of his plan."

"What plan? Whose plan are you talking about?"

"The one who sent me here to help you finish what she started. We can lead you to the first book and the recording she left behind. Finding this book is very important to us, because each soul will return to their rightful owner once their stories are told. Heaven or hell may be their home, but only God knows. Some stories may be hard for you to stomach, while others will bring you to tears. Let me not forget about the ones that will leave your mind in a puzzle, confused, and at the same time still wanting to know how things end. Not only do the victims want their voices to be heard, the killers want the world to know why their hearts have turned cold. We all have life stories, some worse than others. At the end, we all will discover what will make one commit murder."

"Why me? What am I supposed to do with the information?" I asked Peter.

"Take notes and try your best to reach their families, if you can. We all would want to know what happened to our loved ones, wouldn't you?" he asked.

I paused and thought real hard. Then Peter said, "If you were dead, wouldn't you want your family to know what happened to you and who did it?" he asked me in a strong voice.

"Yes, but I'm only twelve," I said to him.

"That makes it even better; they will never believe a child is behind revealing the unknown."

From that day, I agreed to help them, not realizing what was being asked of me. I got dressed and took the books that Ms. Annabelle had given me. Peter led me to the book and the tape recorder as he promised, but he never mentioned that I would have to break into a stranger's home. Once I got in, I stood still, looking around, not quite sure of what I would find. What I did see was very pleasing to my eyes. I saw jewelry, very expensive furniture, and paintings only a person of great riches could afford. Before I knew it, the wrong thoughts had begun to enter my mind.

"The book is what we came for, the book, Joe. Focus," Peter said.

"Where is it?" I asked him.

"In the brick walls."

I pressed every brick until I came across one that moved.

"Stop!" Peter said. "This is the one."

I pulled the brick out and stuck my hand inside. There it was, the book and the tape recorder. As I began to walk away, Peter said to me, "Wait! There's a bag in there. Get it, and let's go."

I grabbed everything that was hidden in the wall, and then I tried my best to put everything back into place. As I dropped down from the window, Peter was standing right there with his hand out.

"What? What do you want?" I asked him.

"The item that you took off the table," he said to me.

I handed him the ring, and then I threw my hood over my head as I walked down the alley.

"Never take what doesn't belong to you. You have plenty. If you just have patience, you'll have more than your eyes have ever seen," he said to me.

"What are you talking about?" I asked him.

"In here," Peter shouted.

"It's dark in there," I protested.

"Come on, Joe, before someone sees you," he urged.

I went even though I was scared. I sat down on a rock and pressed the PLAY button on the tape recorder. This is what I heard.

"This book is one out of the four that were hidden in the walls of the homes of the people who killed me and the others. The town of Oak Steel, where people are killed and the stories go untold. Everyone in the town suffers from a mental illness, a strong hold that rapes you and takes everything that you own. It's hard for me to explain it to you at this time, without you knowing all of the details. Whatever you do, don't throw me away. You will need me more than you could ever imagine. The book is the only way you will be able to find the second tape recorder and the second tape will help you find the next book. I know you're wondering who I am. I will tell you only at the end. What I can tell you is that I used to live here many years ago. I've waited for so long for the chance to be able to tell my side of the story. I tried to explain, but no one would listen to a word I had to say. So I recorded myself and wrote down what I could before that deadly night, hoping someone would pick up where I left off, and here you are. Before I forget, I need to inform you about some of the spirits you may encounter. Some spirits may speak as if they are still living, so never mention that they are dead. Some will become angry if you do, and you may not be able to control them once they are in that state. What state? you may ask. The state of confusion? You will come across others who will flip back and forth from the past to the present, and that's okay. Your job is to remain calm at all times. Keep your emotions in place. I'm not saying you can't cry, because you can. You can scream if you want to, but when it's all done, you must fall back in line and remain focused if you want to make it. You have to make it to the end of the story. You might think that it is easy. However, it's not. Pay close attention and follow the clues step-by-step. Don't worry; I have it all worked out for you. Just follow the steps that are written in the book and listen to what I'm telling you. If you make it, the reward is great. If you don't, I don't know what else to say. You must go now; they are coming. Run, and continue to listen to me as you escape . . ."

I pressed PAUSE on the tape recorder and placed it in the bag. Then I began to walk back and forth. I was scared. *What is going on? I'm ready to throw the book and tape recorder away. I just want to go home. I don't understand what she is talking about.* "I'm only twelve years old!" I screamed out loud.

"So what?" Peter said.

"I want to go home," I said out loud.

"Why do you want to go home? What is there for you?" he asked.

"My family," I said to him.

"What family? A family in which a stepfather rapes you and your siblings and your mother does nothing about it? Is that what you are calling home?" he asked me.

"How do you know?" I screamed with tears rolling down my face.

"I was there," Peter said.

"You watched him do this to me and did nothing?" I yelled.

"I was only doing what I was told," he said to me.

"Who told you to stand still and watch him rape me? These spirits that you and this woman on the tape speak of?" I demanded.

"Right now, you are too young to understand. We must keep moving, Joe. If we do not, we will be seen," he said to me.

"By whom? Who will see us, and who are we running from?" I asked.

"Them, the ones running behind me," he said and then stepped aside.

They were running toward me, making a strange noise. I couldn't stay around to see what they looked like. The only thing that was on my mind was running. I ran into the woods and stood still. I couldn't find Peter. "Peter!" I called, but he never answered.

"I guess I'm next to tell my story," a young girl said to me.

I quickly turned around. *Where did she come from?* I asked myself. She had long brown hair, clear skin, and clean clothes and was holding a doll in her hand.

"Aren't you going to record me and write at the same time?" she asked me.

I just stared at her.

"The other recorder is in the bag," she said to me.

But I didn't answer. I reached into the bag and pulled out the other tape recorder. This one was painted red. I'd had no clue it was in the bag. How did she know? She snatched the tape recorder out of my hand; I backed up and just stared at her.

"Who are you? And what is your name?" she asked me.

I didn't answer her.

"Well, my name is Len."

"What do you want?" I asked her.

"Where's the tape? We need to put it in here, you fool!" she yelled at me.

I reached inside the bag again and pulled out the tape. She took it out of my hand.

"What else is in there?" she asked.

I began walking backward as she started walking toward me. She grabbed hold of my arm and then said, "She is the one," out loud.

"No touching! You know the rules," Peter told her.

"Peter Long, I didn't know you were with her," she said to him and then smiled.

"Let go," he commanded.

"You should never leave her alone," she said to Peter, and then she let me go.

"Tell your story, or move on," he told her.

She handed me back everything she had taken, and then I pressed PLAY. This is what she said.

*　　*　　*

Today is my sweet sixteen birthday. I wanted to celebrate it by having a party, but my parents wouldn't allow it. This caused me to be upset. I refused to talk to them; I even went as far as believing that they would need me before I would need them. In the end, they proved me wrong. After I pleaded my case, my mother did agree for me to have a few friends sleep over tonight. I guessed something was better than nothing. I had so much to do before they arrived. I needed my mother's help, but she and my father had a business dinner they had to attend. I was surprised that my parents would allow us to be left alone. I did believe this could be a test just to see if I could be trusted. If it went well, more freedom would come my way.

I never had the chance to get things in order; before I knew it, my friends began to arrive. Tiffany had been my best friend since the third grade. She was like the big sister I never had, even though she was only three months older than me. I had another best friend named Robyn, but she's no longer with us. No one in this town wanted to talk about it; they acted like she never existed. An eight-year-old died a horrible death, and the police closed the case before it ever began. They had good leads, reliable witnesses, but no arrest was ever made. Who were they trying to protect? I would ask myself that time after time.

Joy and Sherry were out of control. I loved hanging out with them. The laughter and jokes kept my mind off the stressful things that all teen girls went through. Jean was the type of girl who would always tell you the truth even when you didn't want to hear it. There was a time when I picked out this cute outfit and when I tried it on, it made me look like a fat cow. Not even two minutes later, Jean said out loud what I was thinking. What can I say about my friend Laura? You couldn't count on her if something was to go wrong. What I mean by that is, if you were in a fight, you shouldn't look for her to help.

As they began to settle in, my mother called and said for us to order pizza. Then she mentioned that they had to make a stop before coming home. I believed that extra trip was for them to pick up my birthday gift. I hoped they paid close attention to the clues I'd left behind. I wanted a new coat, a leather coat with fur around the sleeves. I would look so good in that coat. As I waited for them to walk in the door with my present, my girlfriends and I were waiting for the pizza to arrive. We needed something to do to get our mind off food. Sherry suggested that we should play games and dance to music. No one wanted to do either. I came up with my own suggestions, which turned out to be worse than Sherry's. I really could have used my mother's help right about then.

As time passed, my guests became bored and hungry. It was so bad that Tiffany took out the dolls that her grandmother had made for us. We were too old to be playing with dolls. Even though I wasn't too thrilled about the gift, I still had to be thankful for it. She didn't have to give us anything. I felt those dolls were scary-looking, but how could I tell my best friend that? I also felt that the dolls were watching me. Their eyes would move from side to side, and then they would stop. About two seconds later, their eyes would move again. Something wasn't right about those dolls. Maybe it was all in my mind or maybe not. We waited and waited, but still there was no food. We became tired of staring at each other. The thought of playing a game did not sound bad after all. Joy had a game in mind.

"What type of game?" I asked her.

"A death game," she answered.

"That's not a game I want to play," Laura said.

"I agree with her!" Tiffany shouted from across the room.

"I don't like to talk about death, so you know I'm not playing that game," I said to Joy.

"Len, you're a scaredy-cat," she said.

"Call me what you want," I replied.

"I'll pass on that one too," Sherry said.

"Okay, I want each of you to answer this question."

"Go ahead, Joy; ask us the question," I said.

"If you should die, what would be the one thing you would want to come back as?"

"I told you, Joy, I don't like to talk about death. We have plenty of time before death starts knocking on the door, anyway," I said.

"Len, answer the question," she said.

I took a deep breath and then said, "If I had to come back as something, I would come back as this doll." That was the only thing I could think of at the time. I thought the question was stupid. We were all sixteen. Why should we be thinking about death? There was so much that I needed to do and think about besides dying. We really needed to change the subject. Before I could change the topic, they all began to answer Joy's question. They repeated the same thing I said and then began to laugh.

"We're just playing with you, Joy!" we all assured her.

"The only thing I know is that when it's time for me to go, I want it to be quick and painless," I said.

"Now can we change the subject, please?" Sherry said loudly.

We started to ask each other questions about the boys we liked in school. Some of the names that were mentioned, I couldn't believe that anyone would have chosen them. As time went on, we began to wonder about food again.

"How long did they say, Sherry?" I asked.

Before she could answer, the doorbell rang. She opened the door, and two men with their faces covered forced themselves in. The door hit Sherry in the face. She yelled, fell to the floor, grabbed her face, and folded into a fetal position. All the screaming made the rest of us turn toward the door. The two men were standing there with guns in their hands.

I stared at everyone. One of the men stood about six feet tall and was wearing a red mask, which covered his entire face except his eyes and mouth. The other man was shorter and wearing a blue mask. Only his eyes showed. I was able to see the skin around their eyes and determine their complexions. The taller man was light-skinned, and his partner was dark-skinned.

"What are you looking at?" the man with the red mask said to me.

I slowly turned my head toward Sherry. I could see the blood running between her fingers. My heart began to skip beats, and my breath was short. The man with the red mask shouted, "Shut up and sit down!" Then he told Jean and me to pick Sherry up. I just stared at him as he repeated his order, this time with a firmer tone. We sat her on the chair, like he told us. Tears started flowing from everyone.

"Please don't hurt us!" Jean said.

"Didn't I tell you to shut up?" he yelled.

"What do you want? The money and the jewelry are in my parents' room," I told them.

"We are not here for that," he said. Then he pointed the gun at me. I just wanted my parents to walk in and help us. Where were they? How long does a business dinner take? I just wanted my mommy.

The man with the red mask yelled, "Everyone upstairs."

"Why? Please, don't hurt us," Jean said to them.

"Jean, let's just do what they say. Everything will be okay," I told her.

"I can't, and you know why, Len," she said to me.

"Pull yourself together; you're going to get all of us hurt," Laura said.

"What's going on over there? Upstairs now!" the man demanded.

"Jean, please, do as they say," Laura said.

"Before I will allow that to happen to me again, I will die," she said.

He walked over and pushed Laura out of the way. The other man with the blue mask just stood between Jean and me. The man with the red mask walked over to his partner and pointed his gun at him.

"Get that gun out of my face," he said.

"So move," he replied.

The man with the blue mask walked over to the staircase and stood.

"Are you going to go upstairs or not?" he said to Jean.

"No!" she yelled.

"You made your choice," he replied.

He shot Jean in the head. Blood splattered all over my face. Everyone began to scream. You could see the smoke coming out of her head. Tiffany and Joy began to throw up. Sherry placed her hands over her mouth to stop herself from screaming, but she couldn't hold back the tears. Laura had her face pressed against the wall.

"If anyone refuses to do what we say, the same thing will happen to them. Now upstairs," he said. I couldn't move.

"Len, let's go," Tiffany said to me. I stood there shaking and crying.

"Move it," he said. I turned around and dug my nails into his eyes. At the same time, I was trying to pull off his mask, but I couldn't get a good grip. Tiffany jumped on his back. The other guy walked over and hit Tiffany in the back of the head with his gun. At the same time, the guy with the red mask managed to break free. I was hit twice in the face with the butt of the gun. He tried to hit me again, but his partner grabbed his arm.

"That's enough!" he yelled.

"What?" he said to him.

"Take the others upstairs, Jay," the man in the blue mask said to him.

Jay, I said to myself. *The one in the red mask is named Jay.*

"I hope you know what you're doing," he said as he walked upstairs.

I lay there with blood running down my face. Right then and there, I started praying to God, asking him to let us walk away from this alive.

"Let's try this again. Get up," he said to me. I stared at his blue mask as I tried to get up. I guess I didn't move fast enough for him. I was kicked in my side, as he repeated the words, "Get up now."

"This is the last time I'm going to tell you!" he yelled at me, right before he stepped on my hand. Laura walked over to the both of us.

"Please, you need to get up," she said to us in a low voice.

Tiffany got up without a problem, but I still couldn't move.

"If you don't get up, Len, he's going to kill you," Laura said to me. As she was helping me, the doorknob began to turn. I screamed, "Run!" and "Go get help!" The one with the blue mask turned around and grabbed me. I reached for his face, and this time, I managed to pull off the mask. His face . . . his face was well known.

*   *   *

Len stopped talking.

"What's wrong?" I asked her as she looked around.

"Do you hear that?" she asked.

"Do I hear what?"

"You should go," she said in a frightened voice.

"Len, what's wrong?"

"They are coming; you really need to go, Joe."

"Will I see you again?" I asked her.

"Yes," she said. "Hurry! Put everything away."

"Who was it that killed you?" I asked, but she didn't answer.

Peter showed up. He grabbed me, and we began running through the woods.

"I'm tired, Peter," I said to him.

"Keep running straight, and don't look back," he ordered.

I did what he said. I kept running, but I had to look back. I needed to see what we were running from. There were four of them surrounding Peter. They were ugly with some type of white foam coming out of their mouths. Their hands and feet were big and long. They had something sticking out of their foreheads. I couldn't tell what it was from where I was standing. Peter turned in my direction and yelled, "Joe, I told you to run and don't stop!"

As soon as I turned around to start running again, something jumped on me. It bit me on the left side of my neck. I managed to push it off me. It was an ugly-looking dog. The dog face was deformed. There was a man sitting there on a rock, and he called the dog back to him. I lay there shaking, blood covering the ground. Peter ran toward me to try to help, but those things were still trying to fight him. Peter called out, "Father, I need your help!" I looked around and saw Peter's help.

Men, women, and children came running toward those ugly creatures. The creatures began to make a noise that hurt my ears. Then I realized they were calling for help as well. As Peter's help started to get closer, the creatures began to look at the man who was sitting on the rock holding the dog. Peter's help and the creatures stared face-to-face waiting for the signal. The creatures took their stand, and a hard covering came over their faces, arms, heads, and backs. While Peter's help drew their swords, the man on the rock yelled something to the creatures, and Peter's helpers called for Jesus. They began to fight.

Peter picked me up and carried me deep into the woods. He took the bag off me and laid me down.

"Am I going to die?" I asked him, but he never said a word.

Peter knelt down and began to pray, just like Ms. Annabelle. He began to speak in another language. Peter got up and touched my neck. I screamed, because I was in so much pain, and then I vomited. I touched my neck and realized the bite mark was gone. There was no trace of blood, not even one sign that I had been hurt.

"We have to go, Joe," he said.

What was wrong with him? I had just been bitten by a crazy-looking animal. "When do we rest?" I asked him.

"Up on your feet now! Move it!"

I got up, and the same man with the dog was standing there.

"Don't look at him," Peter said. "Let's go, Joe."

I put the bag over my shoulder and continued to walk with Peter.

"What is going on? Who is that man?" I asked Peter.

"You ask too many questions, Joe," he said to me.

"I need to know why these things are following us and why that dog bit me. Tell me something. Peter, *talk to me*!" I said to him.

Peter looked at me and then stopped walking.

"What is it that you need to tell me?" I asked him.

"Jesus, help me. Help me to explain this to a child her age," he said.

"Who are you talking to? Who is Jesus?" I asked him.

"Have you ever heard of good and evil?" he asked.

"Yes, but what does that have to do with what is going on?"

"Just listen, Joe, and do not say another word until I'm done. That man and those things that you call creatures are nothing but evil. The right name for those creatures is demons. The man you saw sitting on the rock is one of the chiefs, sent by Satan himself. They are trying to stop what God has called you to do. On this journey, all will be revealed to you. No matter what happens, God is always there with you." And then he paused.

"Something will happen to me?" I asked.

"Quiet," Peter said to me. "Do you hear that?"

"No, I don't hear anything."

"Now do you hear me?" A grown woman appeared from behind the tree.

"Peter," I called in a low voice.

He turned around and asked her, "What is your name?"

She looked at me and then at him. "Why do you want to know?" she asked him.

"What is your name?" he asked her again.

"Suicide," she answered.

Then Peter looked at me. I stood there not knowing what my next move was or why her name was suicide.

"Can I tell my story now, Peter?" she asked.

Peter looked at me and asked, "Are you ready for her?"

"Yes," I said to them both. I took out the recorder and the book. Before she began telling me her story, she wanted me to know about my brother James.

"Your brother James is here with me," she said.

"My brother is with you? Where is he?" I asked.

"Come; let me show you," she said to me.

"Don't listen to her," Peter said to me.

"Why not?" I asked him.

"The devil does nothing but tell lies. He can't tell the truth."

"Who is this devil that you speak of? Does he also go by the name Satan?" I asked him.

She walked over toward Peter and said to him, "This is the child whom your God wants to use against me?"

Peter never said a word.

"She will never make it to the end!" she yelled out loud and then looked at me.

"I'm ready to tell you my story. The young woman before you wrote my story down, but she never had the chance to record it. This is where you fit in."

I reached into the bag and pulled out the book. "Is that your name, Suicide? Am I correct?" I said to her.

"Why should I tell you?" she said to me.

"Without me knowing your name, I won't know which story belongs to you."

"I'm not here to help you; we are not on the same team."

I looked at Peter, and he pointed me back in her direction.

"I'm ready to tell my story," she said to me once again.

I turned on the tape recorder, and she began to speak.

Chapter Two

Enough
The Last Cry

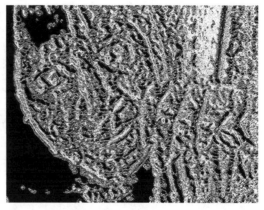

You know the commandments: "Do not murder, do not commit adultery,
do not steal, do not give false testimony, do not defraud,
honor your father and mother."

—Mark 10:19 (NKJV)

"Finally, you reached me. I hope you find my story more interesting than the others. Before we begin, Joe, I have something to ask you. Are willing to listen and answer my questions?" she asked me.

I looked at Peter to see if it was okay. He shook his head yes. "Yes, I will listen and answer your questions."

She smiled and then began to speak. "What would you do if you walked in and saw the person that you love having sex with your son or daughter? Can you even imagine that in any way? You couldn't stomach the thought, but I had to face the truth. I'm about to tell you what I've done. You already know why, but you need to know how my story ended. It will only take about ten minutes of your time."

Even though she was dead, I could still see the pain in her face. I tried to say something to her, but she talked over me. I just remained silent. "Thank you," she said and then continued on with her story.

* * *

I walked in on my husband and son having sex. I knew he was cheating, but I didn't know with whom. The last person I would have ever expected would be my seventeen-year-old son. It seemed like a bad dream I couldn't wake up from. The pain in my heart and the ache in my head is too much for me to bear. This is one moment I wish I could ease. I came home early just to get some rest; I'd been working late for the past three weeks. My body began to shut down; no coffee or energy drink could do the job. Having the house to myself for a few hours, without the kids and my husband, it was a dream come true.

As soon as I walked in, I quickly took off my shoes and flopped down on the sofa. "Finally, I'm here," I said to myself.

As I began to drift off, I heard a moaning sound coming from upstairs. At first, I tried not to pay it any attention. And then I heard the words, "Yes, right there" and "Don't stop." My eyes flew open. I couldn't move fast enough. I stood there at the bottom of the staircase shaking my head, but I knew I had to go upstairs.

I checked every room before getting to my own. I knew where the noise was coming from, but I still took my time. I didn't completely walk in. I stood in the door and peeked. I couldn't move for a few minutes. I was in shock from what I saw. I walked away, went into the den, and began to drink. My son and my husband—"No, no," I repeated as I hit myself on the forehead. Tears followed, because I knew that my family had been destroyed. I don't want to say it, but I was prepared to end it all. Before I did, I needed to write down why I went mad, which I did because you're reading it now. I didn't want the news reporters to get it wrong. Just in case you don't know, just in case you didn't figure it out yet, you're reading my suicide letter. As I was drinking, he walked in.

"Oh, baby, I did not know that you were home. When did you get in?"

He tried to kiss me, but I pulled away. I know where his lips had been.

"Why did you do that? What is wrong with you?" he asked me.

I did not answer. I just stared.

"Did you have a bad day at work? If so, don't take it out on me. Work should never be brought home. How many times must I tell you that, Suzie?"

The more he talked, the more he pissed me off. "Please, just shut up," I told him.

"No, you shut up; who do you think you're talking to?" he yelled.

I had to shake my head and laugh. "Please, Robert, not now," I said to him.

"If you have a problem, we can talk about it, but I won't allow you to keep speaking to me in that way. Do I make myself clear?" he said.

Did he make himself clear? I said to myself. "Robert, you're speaking to me like I'm a child, but that's okay. You're right; I do have a problem," I said. "I want you to sit down and listen if you don't mind."

"Why not? I'm always here for you, my love. You mean a lot to me," he replied.

All this sweet talk was driving me crazy. I took another drink before I began to speak. He sat there with his legs crossed and his hands placed in back of his head. The closer I came to the punch line, the closer I moved toward the desk near the window where he kept his gun. As I pulled the drawer open, he turned around.

"What are you looking for? There's nothing in there but my gun." Then he stood up.

"I know that, Robert. Sit down," I said.

"Suzie, you've been drinking too much. Put the gun down!" he yelled.

"I'm not going to say it again, Robert. Sit down now!"

As he sat down, I walked around the sofa with the gun in my hand. I had to face him; I had to see his expression when I dropped the bomb.

"Suzie, don't point that gun at me," he said.

"Robert, don't you say another word. Only speak when I tell you to, and I mean it," I said.

Finally, he shut up. Now he was wondering, but I stopped talking and just stared at him. Sweat rolled down his bald head. Everything that he had done to me was running through his mind. Not knowing what I actually knew was killing him. I wanted him to sweat; he needed to sweat a little bit longer. "Now I'm ready to talk. Let's talk about you cheating on me," I said to him. He raised his hand so he could speak. For a minute, I thought he was trying to be funny. I totally forgot about what I had told him.

"Yes, Robert, you can speak."

"I'm not cheating on you, Suzie. How many times must I tell you that? You're all that I need in my life!" he shouted at me.

Those words—*You're all that I need in my life*—played over and over in my mind. Then I started to recall the scene with him and my son. My head began to hurt, "You liar!" I yelled and then threw the lamp against the wall. "Stop with the lies!" I told him. "Robert, are you telling me that you have not cheated?" I screamed.

"Suzie, calm down. Tell me what it is that you know? Then we can talk about it. Because I know I have not cheated on you."

I couldn't take it anymore, so I shot him in the leg. Robert yelled.

"Shut up right now before I shoot you again." I cocked the gun, and he instantly shut up and pushed his back against the sofa.

"Suzie, I know you don't want me to speak, but I'm bleeding badly over here. I need to go to the hospital," he said.

I looked at his legs and then said, "That's not a lot of blood. You will be all right. I can't let you go until you tell me the truth."

"I don't know what you want me to tell you. I don't know what you're talking about. Suzie, please tell me what's going on. I'm losing a lot of blood!" he yelled. I looked down again; his left leg was covered with blood. "Suzie, look at me. What did your friends tell you this time?"

I paused and then answered him, "No, honey, my friends didn't tell me anything. Once again, are you cheating on me?" I yelled.

"I'm afraid to answer that question!" he yelled back.

"How could you? Why would you? And how long has this been going on, Robert?"

"How long has *what* been going on?" he screamed.

"You sleeping with our son, you sick bastard!" I shot him once more, but this time in the shoulder.

"Please, Suzie, don't shoot me anymore!" he cried out. "You don't want to kill me. Let me explain!"

"Explain what? How can you explain having sex with your son?" I asked him.

"It just happened, Suzie. I don't know what else to tell you. It just happened."

Tears rolled down my face, and then I yelled, "Things like that don't just happen."

I raised the gun. He tried to jump over the sofa, but I shot him twice in his back.

My son began to bang on the door. "Dad, are you okay? What was that noise? Open the door," he said.

I walked over and stood behind the door as I opened it. He saw his father facedown on the sofa and ran to him. Then I closed the door. Tim turned around and looked at me. "Ma, what did you do?" he yelled. I just looked at him and then shot him in the chest. His body lay right next to his father's. One, two, and three, the gasping for air was no more. I stared at their lifeless bodies. Robert put me through too much. I forgave a lot of things, but this I couldn't. Having sex with our son, could that be considered cheating? I didn't know if it was, but I was tired of him fooling around. I'd had enough, and I wouldn't allow this to be our family secret.

∗   ∗   ∗

"I sat down at the desk and wrote a note to my parents, explaining what had happened. I know they never received it, because I'm sitting here talking to you, Joe. Whatever happened to the letter, only the police know. After I was done writing, I put the gun to my head. There were no bullets left. That would be the quickest way. *What do I do now?* I said to myself. I could cut my wrists or slice my throat. *Who am I kidding?* I wouldn't be able to do that. I sat there and drank some more. I could hear the sounds of law enforcement a few blocks away. As I sat at my desk, I closed my eyes, and before I knew it, they were inside my house. I had the gun placed on my lap. I knew what I was going to do now. I grabbed the gun with my right hand. 'Put the gun down!' one of the officers said to me. I grabbed the note with my other hand. 'Put the gun down,' he said again. I stood up and pointed my gun at them. I don't need to say anymore. You figure out the rest."

Suzie looked at me and then asked, "Did you find me in the book?"

"Yes, I did, 'The Last Cry' story is you."

She smiled at me and then said, "I have to go now."

"Wait! I have a few questions to ask before you go," I said.

"Can I stay?" Suzie asked out loud.

Peter looked at her and shook his head yes.

"Joe, ask your questions," she said to me.

"Why is your name Suicide?" I asked her.

"The name that man gave me was Suzie, but the spirit that claims my life is called Suicide. Now that I'm able to look back, I never had the right to take my life, because my life does not belong to me. It belongs to God. I had no right. I took my life and the lives of others, and it was wrong—no matter what the situation was. I wish I would have handled things differently."

"This suicide spirit, is this of God?" I asked.

"Oh, no. It's of the devil, sent to kill things that belong to God. I believed every word the devil spoke, and it was all lies. I was told that no one loved me and that I would never be anything in life. On the day of my funeral, so many people showed up. I never wanted to cause my family any pain, but I did. I wish I could have done many things differently, but it's too late. I was told, Joe, by a woman standing next to me at the bus stop, 'Choose you this day whom you will serve.' The woman was referring to God."

"This thing called the devil told you nothing but lies and because you believed it, now you're dead?"

"Joe, the devil tells us a lot of things that are nothing but lies; maybe Peter will take the time to tell you more."

"What now?" I said to her.

"Well, Joe, God had a way and a plan to fix what I was going through, but I didn't wait or trust in God," she said.

"I was told that this God is able to do all things, is it true? Have you seen him?" I asked her.

She looked at Peter and then said to me, "Read the book that Ms. Annabelle gave you. It has everything you could possibly need to help you in life," Suzie said. "I really have to go."

"I know you do. Please wait," I said to her.

"Why are you so angry?" I asked her.

"I cheated myself out of life. When I died, I saw how much it hurt my loved ones, and I missed out on a wonderful life that God had for me. I never had the chance to enjoy it. That's why some of us are mad," she said.

"Joe, she has to go. End it," Peter said.

"Okay, Peter," I said.

"Where do you go now that your story is completed?" I asked her.

"Only God knows," she said to me.

"So you have to be judged by this person called God too?" I asked her.

She laughed and then said, "He is more than a person, he is well known. Good and evil know his name. He is the ruler of all things, the one and the only true living God," Suzie said.

"Is that true?" I asked Peter.

He shook his head yes.

"I really have to go, Joe. Please let my family know the real truth behind my death. Before I forget, my husband is the sheriff's brother," and then she disappeared.

Suzie left me with a blank look on my face. *The sheriff is behind a lot,* I said to myself.

"Let's go," Peter said.

"Can you answer a few questions for me, Peter?" I asked him.

"Well, it depends on what it is, Joe," he said to me.

"I want to know more about this suicide spirit that is able to claim people's lives. What does it do? What is its purpose?" I asked.

Peter looked at me in a strange way. I guess he wasn't expecting me to ask him those types of questions. I needed the answer just in case I came across it again. I would know what to do. Peter looked up toward the sky and asked if he could explain it to me. A quick flash of lightning came across the sky.

"What was that? And who are you talking to when you look up toward the sky?" I asked.

"God," Peter said to me.

"God, does he live in the clouds?" I asked him.

"No, not exactly, but let me answer your questions."

I kept quiet while he was speaking. I didn't want to miss anything he had to say, and this is what he told me.

"Joe, people go through stressful life issues, and right now, you might be too young to understand, but I will try my best to answer your questions. Some people are faced with serious financial or relationship problems—in other words, life situations that seem impossible to deal with—but they can overcome those things with the help of God. The devil places negative thoughts in a person's mind. Once the devil is able to take over your mind, he has you. The fight is in your mind. You must fight. You can't give up, Joe. The devil wants you to feel ashamed, guilty; he wants you to think you're a burden to others. He loves to keep you feeling like a victim, just so you will hold on to all the bad things that have ever happened to you in life. When or if that happens, you are trapped in the past and you are not able to move forward unless you let go and forgive the ones who hurt you. You never want to remain stuck in the past because God is not there; he is in the future, waiting for you to seek him so he can help you. We all need to become the man/woman of God that he created us to be. Feelings of rejection, loss, and loneliness also come from the devil. Those feelings can cause a person to commit suicide if they don't seek help," Peter explained.

"Why would a person not want God's help when they are facing hard times?" I asked Peter.

"Some think that they can do it on their own. They don't need anyone's help, especially a God they have never seen and won't take the time to know. The real reason is some people think they don't deserve his help, due to the lifestyle that they are living. Sometimes, we get in our own way of being helped. God wants you to come to him as you are. When he finishes with you, you won't be the same. But you have to seek him, Joe. Seek the kingdom of heaven, and everything else will be provided to you. What is the key word, Joe?" he asked.

"*Seek* is the key word. I'm listening, Peter," I said to him. "It's hard to believe that there is a God who wants to help you that you have never seen, when you have family and friends you see every day and they won't lift a finger to help you. They'd rather watch you drown. I guess that's love?" I said to him.

"No, that is not love, Joe. People are not perfect, but God is and always will be," he said.

"Why can't I see him or hear his voice? Your God doesn't want to talk to me? I'm not good enough for him? Or is it because I'm a girl?"

"You're wrong, Joe. Those last questions that you just asked are all wrong."

I broke down and started to cry. I couldn't take anymore.

"Why are you crying? Don't cry, Joe," Peter begged.

"My life has changed within twenty-four hours; everything that I thought was the truth is nothing but a lie, and the truth is hard for me to believe. Have we all been walking around in a daze? Why have we accepted a life that produces nothing but bad fruit when there is a God who wants to give us things that we could never imagine? Why are we stuck?" I asked.

"Joe, you have been fed lies from the devil himself. We don't belong here; we all have a job to do, and we are sent here by God to complete his will. Some people are afraid of change, so they stay where they are. Others want to change, and when the change doesn't feel good to them, they go back to their old ways. Then we have those who want to change and don't know how, but once they understand that God can help them, they are determined to change no matter what may happen along the way. I'm telling you this, Joe; you must decide which one of those people you will be."

"His will?" I said out loud. "What is that? Ms. Annabelle said something like that. She told the men before they killed her that she had finished what her father wanted her to do. Is the word *Father* another word for God?"

"Yes, that is another word for God. Joe, I also need you to know that we all have a purpose here, and some have died, not knowing what it was," Peter said.

"Really?"

"Yes, it's sad, but true," he said.

"Not knowing your purpose before you die? I don't want that to happen to me. The town I live in is run on a system; no one is willing to make a change, and those who try wind up dead. I tried to tell the other girls who are my age to speak up. I even asked them if they wanted more than what the town was willing to give them. Not even one person, Peter, wanted more. They were comfortable with how things were. I would say to myself, *I know there's more to life than for me just to take orders from a man and have as many babies as he says he wants.* God must have a purpose for me, Peter. What is it? And please don't say it's for me to live like the others in darkness," I said.

"Darkness? You know more than I thought."

"I knew I was different from the others, and I tried my best to fit in, but I wasn't happy living the way Oak Steel wanted us to live. When I met Ms. Annabelle and she began to tell me about your God, I wanted to know more about him, but she didn't have the chance to explain. Why would God let her die?" I asked.

"Joe, there are some questions only God holds the answers to. Sometimes, he will reveal it to you, and sometimes, he won't. That doesn't mean he doesn't love you or he's just being mean. For some things that happen to you in life, it's better that you don't know the reason why."

I just looked at him and thought really hard about what he'd said. I guessed he was right. Sometimes you think you want to know the truth, but when it's revealed, you wish you didn't.

"We have to find shelter," Peter said. We walked and talked until we reached this old house on the hill.

"Where are we? Are we still in Oak Steel?" I asked.

"Yes, we are."

"I've never seen this house here before. Where did it come from?"

"It was always here."

We finally made it to the front door of the house. Peter knocked twice, and someone came to the door and asked for the password. "Love thy neighbor," Peter said. The door opened. I wanted to see what was on the other side of the door . . . then again, I didn't. Peter pushed me forward.

"You're not coming in with me?" I asked him.

"No, I will be back for you in the morning," Peter said.

"No, Peter, don't leave me. I don't want to stay without you."

"Joe, you must go in."

"No, I will be by myself in there. Who will help me if that man shows up?"

"Stop that crying!" he said to me. "It's not about you, Joe. You have a job to do, and that is to fulfill God's will."

"I don't know this God you speak of. So far, I have these creatures following me—and let us not forget they tried to kill me—people from the dead talk to me, and no one else can see them but me."

Before he could answer, I heard a voice saying, "I see them too. You're not alone."

"Who said that? Where are you?" I yelled.

A little boy came out of the house and said, "I see them, Joe."

I just looked at him. He was about my age, very tall, and had red spots all over his skin. I turned around and said, "I can't stay here," but Peter was gone. "Peter!" I yelled out loud.

"I think you should come in; they are coming," the boy said to me.

I looked down the hill toward the woods. "I don't see anything," I said to him.

"Look harder."

I looked again and saw them running up the hill. It was the same creatures, but these were bigger.

"Come on; we have to close the door," he urged. I looked down the hill once again and then went inside.

The boy ran down this long hallway. "Wait!" I said to him, but he never stopped. I found myself standing in the middle of the hallway. "Hello? Where are you?" I said loudly.

He stuck his head out. "I'm right here. Come," he said to me.

I ran in his direction, and when I walked into the room, I couldn't believe my eyes. His room had paintings of a man being beaten.

"Who is this man?" I asked him.

"Don't you want to know my name first?"

"Do you want to tell me? I'm not supposed to ask any questions. I do only when Peter is with me. He's my protection," I said to him.

"Peter Long is not your protection."

"He's not? I don't understand," I said to him.

"God is the one who protects you. He uses Peter to carry out his command. Peter Long should never get the glory, only God."

"I'm sorry; I didn't know. Is your God mad at me now?" I asked.

"Just be careful with giving credit to things or people and not God. He is a jealous God, so always give him the glory, Joe."

"I will," I said.

"Well, since you didn't ask me, my name is David, but people around here call me Dave."

"People around here? There's no one here but us," I said to him.

"Look again," he said.

I closed my eyes and opened them again. I saw them. "They are like the one I saw who came to get Ms. Annabelle. She called them . . ."

"Angels?" Dave said to me.

"Yes, an angel, that is what she said." I started to cry. "They are so beautiful. What are their names? What is their purpose?" I asked Dave.

"Come and sit at the table with me; we will be here for a while."

We sat down, and then he began to talk to me about each one of them and the job God had given them. This is what he said.

"Do you see the angel sitting at the table closest to the door? That angel right there is the one who saved Lot and his family." I looked at the angel not quite sure of who Lot was and the story behind him, but I knew it had to be in the book Ms. Annabelle gave me. So I just stared hoping to get the angel's attention, which I did. The angel turned around and smiled at me. I couldn't help but smile back. Dave leaned over and said, "Joe, sitting on the left side of that angel, we have the angel who protects birds."

"Birds?" I said out loud. "Birds have angels that watch over them too?"

Dave just looked at me, and then he smiled.

"What about the angel who is sitting on the right side of the angel who saved Lot and his family?" I asked him.

"You don't want to know about that one," he said.

"Why not?" I asked him.

He looked at me and then said, "The angel on the right side is the archangel of death."

When I heard the word *death*, my heart started beating very fast.

"Calm down, Joe. Let's move on to the next table," Dave said.

"At table two, the angel who's sitting on top of the table is the angel of the womb."

"Are you saying that this angel protects women's wombs?" I asked him.

"Yes, Joe. The devil attacks the children of God even in the mother's womb."

I just looked at him and then said to myself, *This thing called the devil or Satan is out to destroy everything that is of God.*

"You're right," Dave said.

"How do you know what I'm thinking?" I asked him.

"I don't, but God does and he speaks to me. Then I speak of what the Father tells me," Dave said.

I just looked at him; I had nothing else to say. I just wondered whether I would be able to hear the Father's voice like he did.

"Joe," Dave said out loud, "pay attention."

"I'm sorry; finish," I said to him.

"The angel with its head down; that angel protects infants."

"There are so many angels here. Will I get to know them all?" I asked.

"Yes, you will but not all at once. I'm telling you the ones God wants you to know right now."

"Why must I know only those?" I asked him.

"Only God knows that."

I looked at the ceiling and then back at the angels.

"Joe, let's take a look at the third table. The angel who has his back up against the wall, that angel brought the plague of hail upon Egypt," Dave explained.

"Wait I'm having a hard time following you. I need to know who Lot is and why there was a plague of hail upon Egypt."

He looked at me and then said, "Where are the books Ms. Annabelle gave you?"

I pulled out the books and gave them to him, and then Dave said to me, "This book right here is all that you need, but you must read it for yourself."

"The book has a lot of pages, and I don't understand what I'm reading."

"Joe, you haven't tried to learn what's in the book. I know what's in there and so does the devil. This book is for you. I can't make you read it, but I will say this: If you want to make it to the end, you must rely on God, have faith, and believe in his words, Joe. You cannot defeat the enemy with your own words, only with the words of God."

"There are so many rules on this side. Why can't I just play with baby dolls and call it a night?"

Dave busted out laughing. I just looked at him.

"Are you surprised?"

"Yes, I didn't think you were allowed to laugh or have fun."

"Joe, doing things God's way is not a punishment. You need to look at it as being the best way of living."

"Dave, I just need you to listen to me and don't say a word until I'm done."

Dave looked at me and nodded. I began to express myself. "I was awakened by a dead man; then Peter Long showed up and brought a few dead folks along with him. Silly, I agreed to go with Peter to finish a job of a dead woman that I never met. Being on this journey, I have run into creatures and demons. Then I was bitten on the neck, facing death, but Peter prayed to your God and touched my neck; by the way, it hurt like you-know-what. On top of that, I'm talking to these sprits who really want to kick my butt, but they can't because your God has me protected. Now I'm sitting here with you talking about angels. They are very lovely, but I still have not met this God of yours. So I don't see how this is a better life." I said to him.

Dave and all the angels started laughing.

"I don't see what's so funny!"

One of the angels stood up and said, "Come; touch my hand, and see what others have gone through. Then you can answer your own questions."

"Why is this angel speaking to me?" I asked Dave.

"No, speak to me; I'm the one who's talking to you," the angel said to me.

"I just wanted to know what kind of angel you are," I said to him.

"I am the angel of visions; now touch me."

I reached out my hand, and then I was pulled right in. I watched a mother holding her child's hands while she was dying in a hospital bed. Then I saw children laughing and playing even though some of them were missing an arm or a leg. There were some who had been born with neither, and they still had smiles on their faces. As soon as I was able to get a closer look, the angel brought me to a country where the people drank and bathed in the same water the animals placed their waste into. "Don't drink the water; you will get sick!" I said out loud, but they couldn't hear me. I was also shown young girls my age being tied to a bed and different men coming in and out of the room. They were held captive in this sex trade. Some were crying, while others seemed like they had been drugged, not knowing what was going on. Then everything slowed down and went dark.

"What's going on?" I asked.

"Be quiet," the angel said to me.

"Why are we in this house?" I asked. The angel never answered.

The more we walked, the lighter it became. A man came in the front door holding his head.

"It hurts. Please help me, Jane!" he called.

She came running down the steps. "What's wrong?"

"I can't take no more. It hurts; the voices are too much!"

She ran to the table and grabbed a pill bottle. "Take your meds," she said to him.

"Get those meds away from me!" he yelled.

"Please take them, C.J.," she said.

He walked to the closet by the door and pulled out a gun.

"C.J., what are you doing?"

"This is the only way I can stop the voices, Jane."

"Please put the gun down, C.J.!" she yelled.

"Do you see them? They are crawling all over me!"

I began to look to see if I could see what he was talking about, and I did. I screamed, and the angel covered my mouth. C.J. put the gun in his mouth, and it went off. Jane was screaming and yelling while she held him in her arms. I could not believe what I was seeing. Something came out of him. I started screaming and yelling; the angel quickly brought me back.

I pulled away and began screaming, "You stay away from me. Why would you show me that? Why?" I grabbed my books.

The angel said to me, "Where do you think you're going?"

"I'm leaving!" I yelled.

The door and the windows slammed.

"You can't keep me here!" I screamed.

"Calm down, Joe," Dave said to me.

I opened the door and saw the demons waiting. I turned around and said, "Well, I changed my mind."

Everyone started to laugh again.

"Come, Joe; I have more to show you," Dave said.

We walked inside a room where there was nothing but paintings covering the walls.

Dave pointed to the picture where the man was being beaten.

"Who is this man?" I asked Dave.

"His name is Jesus. He is the son of God, the word wrapped up in flesh, the messiah, master, or the chosen one."

"So many names for one person," I replied.

"You just don't know."

"Can you explain to me what is going on in these pictures?" I asked him.

"Where do you want me to begin?"

Right when I was about to tell him where to start, I heard a little girl laughing.

"Who's there? Is there someone else here with us, Dave?"

"Don't be scared, Joe," he said.

She laughed again.

"Who's there? And where are you?" I demanded.

"Don't be scared, Joe," Dave said to me once again.

"Show yourself now, in the name of Jesus!" Dave said out loud.

"No, please stay where you are. Dave, let's get out of here, please," I said to him.

"You can't be afraid of them; they feed off your fear, Joe."

"I don't want to see anything else tonight. I just want to get something to eat and go to sleep," I said to him.

"Warriors never sleep," he said to me.

"Who is a warrior? I just learned how to read. How can I be a warrior?" I said to him.

"May I show myself, David?" she said out loud.

"Yes," he answered. I stood behind Dave not knowing where she would appear.

She came crawling down from the ceiling, and I took off running.

"Joe, don't run!" he yelled.

I ran back toward the front door. Peter was standing right there. I ran toward him.

"Peter, please, we have to get out of here," I said to him.

"What did you see?" he asked.

"I don't know what she was, Peter," I said to him.

"I can't do it. Have your God choose someone else. The woman was right; I'm not the right one for the job," I said to him.

Peter looked at me and lifted me up. He started walking toward the room.

"No, I don't want this! I don't want this!" I yelled all the way down the hallway. Before I knew it, we were inside the room.

"Show yourself. Where are you?" Peter said out loud.

"I'm right here."

And there she stood. I closed my eyes and held tight to Peter's hand.

"What is your name?" Peter asked her.

She stood there making a groaning sound.

"What is your name?" Peter said, this time in a firmer tone.

"I heard you the first time, Peter," she said to him. "My name is Tammy."

"What do you want? And who sent you here?" Peter asked her.

"Peter, you know I'm not able to come in here without getting your God's permission. I'm here because I was told she was the one I should come to if I want my story to be told. Was I told the right thing?" she asked him.

But Peter never answered. "Who sent you?" he asked.

"What's with all of these questions, Peter, you already know. Why put me through all of this trouble, Peter?" Tammy said to him.

Peter looked at me and said, "Are you ready, Joe?"

"Ready for what?" I asked him.

"Focus, Joe," he said to me.

"I'm trying, Peter. Why are you bringing these things back to me? I have learned how to block them out, and I want it to stay that way," I said to him.

"Joe, just because you refuse to see them does not mean they are not there. You have control over them. God gave you the power and the authority, but you must use it," Peter said.

"Fear is what I see and smell. You're scared of us, and we are the weak ones. I can't wait for you to meet the others," Tammy said to me.

"Shut up. Quiet in the name of Jesus right now," Peter said to her. "Joe, I need you to listen to me. God is always with you. When you are in trouble, call on Jesus's name. Say, 'The blood of Jesus is against you.' Whatever is going on, it will have to stop. There is power in the name of Jesus. Call on him, and you will see," Peter said as he walked away.

"Peter," I said, "please stay. Don't go! Don't leave me!"

"Stop that crying. I didn't come for that; I came to tell my story," Tammy said to me.

I just looked at her and wiped my face with my shirt.

"Hurry up, because my time is almost up. I want to tell you my story before . . ." and then she stopped speaking.

"Before what, Tammy?" I asked her.

"Before I show up? Is that what you were going to say?" she said to Tammy.

"Who are you? And what is your name?" I asked. But she never answered.

I asked the questions again, but she never said another word. Tammy just looked at me and then at it, and they began to laugh.

"I can't do this, Peter!" I screamed.

"You have to use Jesus's name, Joe," Dave said to me.

"Dave, where did you come from?" I asked him.

"Don't worry about me. Say it," he said.

"Who are you? And what is your name? In the name of Jesus, you must answer me," I said to her.

They both stopped laughing, and she looked at me.

"Murder is my name. Now are you happy? I just left the body of a man named Teddy Small. He was on death row, and now he's dead. I'm looking for another body to make my home," she said to me.

"I don't understand. People's bodies are your home? Is that what you're telling me?" I asked.

"Yes, and when the body is full and no more unclean spirits can enter, the body has become our home," she said to me.

"No, you're lying; that can't be true," I said.

"Dave, tell her," she said. But Dave never answered.

"How do you get inside of them?" I asked.

"You don't know, really? Can I tell her?" she said.

"Who are you talking to when you speak out loud? I know you're not speaking to me," I said to her.

"Your God is who I'm speaking to at this moment. We can't do anything without getting the okay from him. Some of you make it easy for us by sinning, going against the things that are of God, and within that sin you have given us an opening to come on in. With others who claim that they love God so much, we in return request for their faith to be tested. Some do pass, and others fail," she said to me.

"I don't know if you're telling me the truth. When Peter comes, I will ask him," I said.

"As for Dave, we have known each other since Adam and Eve . . . even before that. Joe, I really need to tell my story. I have to be the first spirit there when Cynthia sleeps with her boss. He's a married man. The first spirit in rules," she said to me.

"I need to finish things with Tammy first, and then we can talk more," I said.

"Tammy won't mind me going before her. Right, Tammy?" the Spirit of Murder said to her.

I looked at Tammy, and then she said, "I just spoke about there being others that are stronger than the ones you came across and this one here is stronger than me," she said.

"No, Tammy, that might be the way it works on your end, but I was told that I have the power and the authority, so things will go the way I say," I said to her.

"Who the hell do you think you're fucking with?" the Spirit of Murder said, and threw one of the pictures down off the wall.

I moved back.

"Don't be scared, Joe," Dave said to me.

"I have to stand up to her," I said to myself. "Be quiet or just leave," I said to her.

"You think you can beat me? You don't know what you have gotten yourself into," she said to me.

"No, you don't know," I said back to her. "Tammy will go first, like I said. Tammy, I'm ready. Are you?"

"She can go. I'm not in a rush to be sent back to the pit of hell," she said to me.

"The pit of hell, what is that?" I asked Tammy.

"It's hot down there; that's why we fight to stay in the bodies of the ones we have taken over," she explained.

"So you know where you're going once you tell your story?" I asked.

"Oh, yes, back to hell; that's where we came from. Like Murder said, we have been here since Adam and Eve. We know the Bible too and very well. Better than those who claim they do," Tammy said.

"Let Tammy tell you her side, and then she must go. It's getting crowded in here, and we haven't made it to the first family yet," Dave said to me.

I looked around and could see the sprits appearing in and out. It scared me for a second; I had never seen so many, and they all wanted to talk me. *When will I get rest?* I asked myself.

"Okay, I will let her begin," I said to Dave. This is what Tammy had to say.

Chapter Three

Tammy/The Voices

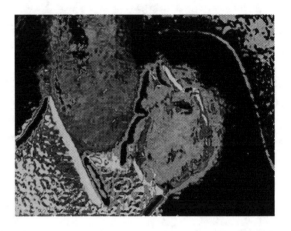

Can

You

Help

Me?

And also some women who had been cured of evil spirits and diseases: Mary (called
Magdalene) from whom seven *demons* had come out . . .

—Luke 8:2 (NKJV)

I woke up with one arm chained to the bed. The rest of my body was placed on the floor. My
eyes were burning; I could barely see. With my free hand, I rubbed my face. There was a knot
on my forehead, three cuts on the left side of my cheek, and two on the right. *What happened
to me?* I said to myself. As I touched my head, I could tell my hair was missing in some spots.
There was also a long cut going across the back side of my head. I began to panic, which caused
me to check my whole body. There was a long tube placed between my legs. I followed the tube
to where it ended, which was inside of me. I tried to pull it out, but it hurt too bad. As I moved, I
felt a warm bag beside me. Without being able to see and with the panic attack, it was very hard

for me to breathe. *You have to calm down,* I said to myself. I tried to get up, but my legs were too weak. For some reason, I could tell that I wasn't alone. I struggled with my vision; every object seemed blurry to me. I heard something drop from across the room. I jumped and turned my head toward the sound. "Who's there?" I asked, but no one answered. I saw something white standing in the corner. I closed my eyes and then reopened them, just to make sure I was seeing what was actually there. It was nothing but a white jacket hanging from a coatrack, I think. The walls had bloodstains, and the floors were dirty. Underneath the table, there seemed to be a human skull. "Help me! Hello?" I yelled. "I know someone is in here with me; please talk to me."

"Tammy," a voice called.

The sound of the voice was behind me. I tried to focus my eyes in that direction, but I still couldn't see the man who was calling me. "Where am I? And why am I chained to this bed?" I asked. I waited, but he never answered me.

"Mommy!" I yelled.

"Stop that damn screaming; no one can hear you, Tammy," he said.

"Who are you? Why am I here? Please answer me." I waited for him to speak again, but he didn't say another word. I couldn't take it anymore. I was beginning to lose my mind. "Hello? I know you're there! Answer me! What have you done to me?" I yelled.

"Shut up right now, Tammy," he said to me.

"Please, just let me go. Whatever I've done, I'm so sorry. I just don't understand why you would do this to me," I said to the stranger. Something was slammed against the wall. "What was that?"

"What was what?" he said.

"I know you heard that. Please stop toying with me."

"Never that, sweetheart, never that." Then he laughed.

I don't know why, but I had to ask again. "What have you done to me?"

"No, you mean what have you done to yourself?" he said.

"Why would I do this to myself?" I yelled.

"I don't know; you tell me."

"Just let me go, and I won't tell anyone what happened."

"I can't do that right now," he replied.

"Someone, please help me!" I yelled.

Before I knew it, he hit me across my face. My face slammed into the edge of the bed, which caused the top of my eyebrow to open. I lifted my head and said, "Do you feel better? By hitting me, does that make you a man now? Answer me, you little bitch!" Then I spit on the floor. He walked over and wiped my face. "Don't touch me," I said to him, and then I spit again.

This time, it landed in his face. "You spit in my face, you little bitch," he said loudly.

I tried to back away, but he stepped on my leg and pulled out the tube that was inside me. I screamed like never before. Blood was everywhere. He placed his hand over my mouth. "Shut up right now! Do you hear me, Tammy?"

How could I when the pain was out of control. The only thing I could do was place my body against the bed and take deep breaths until the pain stopped. I no longer cared if I lived or died. *He's going to kill me anyway.* So I said what I wanted. It was time for me to pick his brain. The next sentence that came out of my mouth was: "I wonder if you get off by seeing others in pain." He moved closer to me. I jumped, figuring he was going to hit me, but he just removed the hair from my face. Then he pulled up a chair and sat right in front of me.

"What the hell do you want from me?" I asked.

He responded by saying, "We won't get anywhere with you using that type of language."

"What language are you referring to?" I asked.

"Don't play games with me. I'm here to help you, Tammy. We can make this stay pleasant, or we can make it very uncomfortable!" he yelled.

As he was talking, I began to regain my vision. "I can see you clearly now," I said.

"That's good to know. Now we both know what we look like." Then he laughed.

"Can I ask you a few questions, mister?"

"No," he said, and then he stood by the door.

From his body language, I could tell that he was going to make it very difficult for me. But I still chose to ask the questions anyway. "What is your name?"

"You don't need to know that," he said.

"So I'll call you mister for now. Why am I here once again?"

He turned around and hit his hand on the door. He said, "I'll be the one asking the questions around here, and you'll provide me with all the answers that are needed."

"Really?" I said to him. "Is that how it's going to go?"

"Yes," he answered.

I stared at him, and he stared at me. Out of nowhere, he picked up a cup from the table and threw it at me. Whatever was in the cup didn't smell too good.

"I can't believe you did that. How could you? You threw piss on me, you asshole!" I yelled at him. "Wait until I get loose, you will pay for what you're doing to me."

"How will you make me pay, Tammy, like the others?"

"I don't know what you're talking about, mister, and you don't either. Why are you such an asshole?" I said to him.

"Watch your mouth. How many times must I tell you about your mouth, Tammy?"

"If I don't stop, what are you going to do to me?" I asked.

"I'll give up on you, and then you'll be left alone in here," he said.

"Where is here?" I asked him.

"I can help you when you help me, not before."

"How can I help you if I don't know what it is that you want?"

"Tell me what I need to know, and I will let you go," he replied.

"If I don't, what will happen to me?" I asked.

He slammed his fist on the table and yelled, "It's easy; it's so plain to see that you'll be in here as long as it takes."

"What are you talking about?" I asked again.

"Please don't act like you don't know, Tammy."

"If I knew, mister, would I be asking? Think about that, asshole!" I screamed.

"Such a dirty mouth for a young girl. You need to be honest with yourself," he said.

I couldn't believe what was going on; the only thing I could do was laugh. While I was laughing, he just stared at me. After a few seconds, I stopped, and then I began to speak again. "The things you want to know, the things I'm about to tell you, mister, you will never believe," I said to him.

He just looked at me and said, "I'm here to help you, not hurt you."

I responded by saying, "I'm not worried about you hurting me, mister. I'm worried about the others that will hurt me."

"The others, who are they?" he asked.

"The ones that you want to know about, that's why you're here. I don't want to talk about them right now. When are people going to focus on me?" I asked him.

"We are focusing on you," he said to me.

"You're a damn liar. You want the information that I could provide for you."

"Okay, I will promise you this, Tammy. You can tell me what you want me to know, and when you're ready to stop, we can."

"You promise. Do you mean what you say, mister?"

He looked down at the floor and then lifted his head up and said, "I do, Tammy." He smiled at me.

I didn't believe him, not even for one second, but I did think it was time for him to see what was in store. I paused for a moment and then said, "Mister, I just want you to know that once I begin, there is no turning back and I'm not accountable for others' actions or reactions. Do I make myself clear? And do you agree with these terms?"

"Yes, I do, Tammy."

"I hope you know what you're asking for," I said to him. "Since you agreed, I want to take you back to when I was seven years old. My father would go off to a hard day of work. He was a police officer; everyone in town loved him, but they all knew that he was too good for my mother. When he would leave for work, she would have different men coming in and out of the home. It didn't matter the color, body type, height, or even their looks. The only thing that mattered was the size of the man pole, how well he could use it, and how good the tongue game was. I would count the men just to see how many in one day. As time went on, I lost count. 'How much can a woman take in one day? It has to be sore down there,' I would say to myself. Those men had to be just as nasty as my mother; I knew she had to smell. I don't think she had time to bathe between each man. I hate to say it, but my mother was a whore.

"My father never knew what was going on—no, correction, he didn't *want to believe* that it was true. One day, he came home early. I knew she was going to get caught. Deep down inside, I wanted her to. There was no way she was going to get away with it this time. She heard the door unlock. He hurried up and grabbed his belongings and jumped out of the window. She ran downstairs to greet my father at the door. He grabbed ahold of his gun and asked if there was someone in the house. 'No, no one was in here, Michael,' my mother told him. He could tell that something wasn't right—the look on her face, her clothing hanging off her body, and her hair all over her head . . ."

*   *   *

"Hold on, I'll be right back; this asshole wants to stop me right in the middle of my story."

I pressed PAUSE on the tape recorder and asked Dave what was going on. He looked at me and then said, "Watch and see. There are some things you have to find out on your own."

"What's wrong, Tammy?" I asked her.

"I'm sorry, Joe, but there are others who are part of this story. Can they come and tell their part?" she asked me.

"I don't know about that right now. I can only deal with one of you at a time, and once you're finished, she goes."

"They only want to tell their story," Tammy said to me.

"Where are they?" I asked her.

"Right here next to me. They are the reason why I stopped, and I will keep stopping because they all are trying to talk to me at once. It's very hard to speak when you have others speaking at the same time," she said to me.

"Do they look like you or like her?" I asked Tammy.

"Just invite them, and then you will see," Tammy said to me.

"Why can't they just show themselves like you did?" I asked her.

"It's not that easy. Some spirits have to be invited in. You have to give the devil access," she said to me.

"The devil? Who or what is that?" I asked her.

"She doesn't know about the devil?" Tammy said to Dave.

Dave never answered her.

I just looked at Tammy and then said, "No more at this time. Finish your story, so I can hear what happened to her, and then I will leave," I said to her.

Tammy turned to them and repeated what I had said to her. They became very angry. I heard a big bang, and then one of the pictures fell off the wall. "You made them and Tom mad," Tammy said to me, and then she continued on with her story.

*   *   *

My father turned and looked at me. He then asked, "Tammy, was there someone in this house?"

I looked at her and then at him. *Why must I be put in the middle?* "No," I said. I know you're wondering why I didn't tell him. Think about it; if I had, my mother would have dealt with me later. By telling my father, what would be the use? He wasn't going to leave her. It had been going on for so long, why would it stop now? Things would never change unless my father decided he had enough and backed up what he said.

As time went on, the same man who jumped out of the window began coming to see my mother every night, even when my father was there. He was scary looking and always talking to himself. He would tell my mother that the dead wanted to take over his body. My mother would laugh and then say, "No one is after you," and "The dead do not want to take over your body." He would get angry and then start mumbling things, which she could not understand. I know you're wondering how often this would happen. It happened so many times that I lost count. The stranger would play with me, call me his baby girl, and tell me how much he loved me. The longer he stayed around, the more I became comfortable and that scary stranger didn't exist anymore. Actually, I started to like Stan. He was very sweet to me, when the voices weren't around. He would ask if I heard the voices. A few times, I would say, "Yes." I didn't want him to think that he was crazy, which he was. But I needed him to be sane around me.

My mother would leave us alone time after time. I would sit there and watch him fight with himself—well, I should say fight with all of the voices that lived inside of his head, that is. It had gotten to the point that it wouldn't bother me because he was always cursing someone or something out, especially, a boy named Tom. Tom wanted Stan to finish something for him. Stan would tell him no. When he didn't listen, for some reason, I felt that Tom took over his body. I don't know why, but it seemed that way to me.

*   *   *

"Wait a minute! I knew a boy named Tom," I said to Tammy.

"Pause the tape," Dave said to me.

"You did?" Tammy said. "Give him the okay, and he will come right over."

"Is Tom with you right now?" I asked her.

"Yes," Tammy said to me.

"Joe, don't listen to her. Never make deals with the devil," Dave said to me.

"But . . . I know Tom. I just wanted to know if he was okay," I said to him.

"You don't know if he's really there," Dave said to me.

"Do you want to see him or not?" Tammy said.

"Say, 'Yes!' Please, say, 'Yes!'" the other spirit said out loud.

"Don't do it, Joe," Dave said to me.

"No, not this time," I said to Tammy.

"Mind your damn business, Dave!" Tammy said to him.

Dave never answered her.

"Please finish the story; I really have to go," I said to Tammy.

"Okay, Joe, where was I . . ."

*   *   *

One day, the voices were so bad that he locked himself inside the bathroom for hours. I had to go. I knocked on the door.

"You wait," he said.

I heard a voice that time. I heard it. "Stan!" I yelled.

"Who is Stan?" the voice screamed as Stan passed me. I ran into the bathroom and stayed there, pacing back and forth. *I can't believe she left me with that crazy man. What am I going to do? If he comes in here, he's going to kill me. Why would he want to kill me? No, I'm too young to die. That voice, what was that voice? Did I really hear it? No way, Stan has to go. He's driving me crazy.*

Finally, my mother returned home. I could hear her calling me. "Tammy, Tammy," she said. I came downstairs, and Stan was sitting there on the sofa.

"Come here, baby girl," he said to me.

"Mother, please, make him leave."

"What is wrong with you?" she asked.

I was so afraid to talk. She looked at him and then said, "Stan, it's about time for you to go anyway, you-know-who's about to come home."

"That's fine," he said. The phone rang, and she went into the kitchen. Stan stood up and said, "Bye, baby girl." I just looked at him. When he walked toward the door to leave, I saw a face poke out of his back.

*   *   *

I had to press PAUSE; I could not believe what I had just heard. "You saw what? You saw a face? How sure are you?" I asked Tammy.

"I'm very sure of what I saw," she said.

I stood up and said to Dave, "It's too much. Is this real?"

"I will explain all of it to you later," he assured me.

"Why not now?" Tammy said to him.

Dave never answered Tammy.

"How come you never answer her questions, Dave?" I asked him.

"Yes, why is that?" Tammy said to him.

"She is trying to confuse you, Joe. I was sent here by God to help you," Dave said to me.

"God? Who is this God? Have you seen him, Joe?" Tammy asked me.

"No, I have not," I said to her.

"Where is he, Dave? How come she can't see him? Answer, Dave," Tammy said.

"You shut up right now in the name of Jesus," Dave said to her.

Tammy placed her hand over her mouth.

Dave pulled me into the hallway. I could hear them laughing.

"Do you hear how they are laughing at you? You have to stay focused," Dave said.

"I'm trying, but it's hard to process it all," I said to him.

"Finish up in there, so we can go and get something to eat," he said.

I agreed, and we walked back inside.

"Yes, let's finish up, so you two can go eat," Tammy said to us.

"How did you hear what we were saying out there?" I asked Tammy.

"We hear everything. Isn't that right, Dave?" Tammy said to him.

"Let's end your story, Tammy," I said.

"Okay, don't be so pushy," she said.

*   *   *

One night, I woke up to moaning and screaming sounds. I walked toward my mother's bedroom. I peeked and there she was lying across the bed. At first, I didn't see anyone else, but then a head moved up and down toward her private area. I always wonder, still to this day, what he was doing to my mother. Anyway, she began to push his head farther down. His head began to move from side to side. She threw her legs around his neck, and he gripped her hips tightly. "Yes! Yes!" she yelled. He stood up and climbed on top. The next thing that I saw was something shaped like a stick or pole that went between my mother's legs. His body began to move. "Faster! Faster!" she said. Sweat was rolling down his face and back. Her legs locked around his waist, and there was screaming and yelling from both.

The young man turned her over, and before I knew it, we locked eyes. "Go to your room!" she yelled. I ran to my bedroom and got underneath the covers.

A few minutes later, my mother entered the room. She began beating me with the belt.

"You want to spy on me?" she screamed. Then I was hit in the middle of my back.

"I'm sorry. Please don't hit me no more, Mommy!" I yelled and then began to cry.

"Don't cry now, you little bitch. Shut it up, and I mean now. You think you're better than me?" she yelled. "Tammy, are you judging me? Answer me!"

"No, Mommy!" I told her.

"Yes, you are. I don't know why I stay around here."

"I'm sorry, Mommy."

"Sorry for what?" she asked.

I never answered, but I did say, "I just want you to stop mistreating me."

"It's not all about you!" she yelled. "What about me, Tammy?"

"I didn't do anything to you!" I said to her.

"You never do anything wrong!" she screamed. Then she hit me again, this time in the face. The belt split the right side of my face.

"I'm bleeding, Mommy!" I yelled at her.

"I don't give a damn." And she swung again.

I crawled underneath the bed to get away from her.

"Get from underneath there now!" she yelled.

"No! I want my daddy!" I told her.

"If it was up to me, you wouldn't be here. Get from under there right now, Tammy."

I didn't move, and she flipped the bed over. I tried to run for the door. She swung; the metal buckle caught me in the back of the head. My face hit the doorknob. I saw Stan from the corner of my eye. "Stan, help! Please make her stop!" He walked over to me, and then I passed out.

* * *

"What happened when you came to?" I asked Tammy.

"Okay, it's my turn; you have taken up enough of her time," the Spirit of Murder said to Tammy.

"I'm not done with her. I have a few questions I need to ask her," I said.

"She's done with you for right now; isn't that right, Tammy?"

"Yes," Tammy said to me.

"No, it's not right. Tammy, don't go," I said to her.

"I have to, Joe. She's stronger than I," she said to me.

"Stronger than you are? I don't understand," I said to her.

"There's a lot you don't know. I can't believe you're the one that God has chosen. I think he made a mistake," the Spirit of Murder said to me.

Before I could answer, Peter entered the room.

"God never makes a mistake, and you know that," Peter said.

"Peter," I said, "where did you come from?"

"Yes, Peter, where did you come from?" the Spirit of Murder asked him.

"We have to go, Joe," Peter said to me. I began to pack up my things.

The Spirit of Murder said to Peter, "She not leaving. I haven't told my story."

"It wasn't your time to speak. Tammy wasn't done," Peter said.

"You don't know the rules on this side," the spirit said.

"I don't," Peter said.

The Spirit of Murder turned around and yelled, "Tammy, I need you to finish the story and make it quick. And as for you two, you make me sick," the spirit said, as she sat in the chair that was against the door.

"You have questions for me?" Tammy asked.

"Yes, I do," I told her.

"I can only answer four for right now," she said to me.

"Will we see each other again?" I asked her.

"Yes, Joe. I have to finish my story, but I do have to go," she said to me.

"Okay, I do understand, so I will ask you my three questions and then you can go," I said. "Did your mother kill you?"

"No, I didn't die by her hands," she said to me.

"Okay, hum, what was the doctor's name?" I asked.

"His name was Carl Smith."

"Carl Smith, the doctor who lives down the hill?"

"Is that your last question?" Tammy said to me.

"No, don't answer that," I said to her.

"Did you ever find out where you were?" I asked instead.

"Yes, but the name I can't give you right now," she said as she walked away.

"Why not, Tammy?" I asked her.

"That's the fifth question," she said to me, and she disappeared.

"Are you finished writing, because it's my turn to tell my story?" the Spirit of Murder said.

"No, we are done," Peter said loudly.

"Peter!" a voice called.

Peter looked at me and then said, "Please, forgive me, Father," and he bowed his head.

"Now that we have that settled, Peter, Joe, turn to a clean page and start the tape. I have a story to tell," the spirit said.

Chapter Four

Alone

Come

Keep

Me

Company.

And ye shall be betrayed both by parents, and brethren, and kinsfolks, and friends; and some of you shall they cause to be put to death.

—Luke 21:16 (NKJV)

Now, it's my turn. Who would ever imagine that one wrong turn would land me in front of a house of hell? Allow me to explain how it all began. I made a wrong turn off the highway, because I wasn't paying attention. I was so in tune with the songs that were being played on the radio that I got off too soon. I tried to find a way to get back, but there were no signs leading back to the highway. I began looking for a gas station, thinking maybe someone there would be able to help me, but none was insight. I had to make it to my aunt's house before it got dark. I drove to this white house. Maybe someone there would be able to help me, I thought. *Here comes help right now.*

"Can I help you?" the man said.

"I'm trying to find Ridgewood Road. Can you tell me where that is?" I said to him.

He smiled and walked over to the car. He was a nice-looking young man, clean-cut and with a nice body. From the looks of things, if he lived there, he had to be doing very well for himself.

"I can show you if you like," he said to me.

"No, that's okay. Just point me in the right direction, and I will take things from there," I replied.

He leaned over and whispered, but I couldn't hear what he was saying. So I asked him to repeat himself.

"I'm sorry," he said to me.

"You're sorry? What are you sorry for?" I asked him.

"You need to be on your way before my father sees you. Make a right at the end of this road," he said.

I didn't know what he meant by that, but I didn't wait to find out. "Thank you," I said and then drove off.

Before I could make it to the next town, I was pulled over by a police officer. He walked up to the car and told me to get out. As I got out, I noticed it was the same young man I had met at the house.

"Did I do something wrong?" I said to him.

"I tried to help you, but you didn't leave fast enough," he said to me.

"What are you talking about?" I asked him.

Before he could answer, a truck pulled up in front of me.

"Is she the one?" he asked him.

"She doesn't know anything. She was just lost; that's all, Father," the younger man said to him.

"Bobby, is she the one?" he asked again.

Before Bobby could answer, I said to the older man, "I'm sorry; I never meant to do anything that would offend you."

"What did you see?" he asked me.

"I didn't see anything. I never got out of the car. Can you please tell him that, Bobby?" I said.

"I tried to help you. I'm sorry . . . Run!" he yelled.

"Run!" I said to myself. *What is Bobby talking about now?*

Bobby's father opened the back of the truck, and two big dogs came out. "You have to the count of twenty before these dogs cut loose." I took off running. I could hear him counting out loud with every step that I took. "Twenty!" he screamed. I kept running and never looked back. Thank God that I ran track. I could hear the dogs running behind me, barking loudly and with the owner yelling, "Kill her!" I saw a barn not too far ahead.

I ran inside the barn, hoping to catch my breath. It was so dark, I couldn't see a thing. "Help me, please," a voice said. I stopped and bent down, waiting to hear it speak again, and I did.

"Hello? Who's there? Talk to me, please. I know someone is here because I can hear you breathing. Get me out of this box before he comes back." I got up and began to move around. I couldn't see the box at first, but my leg bumped into it.

"There's a lock on it," I said.

"I know that. Find something to break it!" the voice said to me.

I tried to feel my way around, but I kept bumping into things. "Why are you making so much noise? Be quiet! Do you want him to hear you? Do you want both of us to die?" the voice said.

"I'm trying. It's hard for me to find anything in the dark," I said.

"You don't want the lights on; you won't be able to handle what you will see," the voice said to me.

"There's nothing here that I can use," I said out loud.

"What do you mean there's nothing here that you can use? Please help me. Don't leave me here alone!" the voice said.

"What is your name?" I asked.

"Sage," she answered.

"My name is Corey," I told her. "Why are you locked in this box?"

"Does that matter right now? Why should I tell you when I don't even know who you are? You could be Old Man Stevens's sidekick for all I know!" Sage yelled.

"The old man's name is Stevens?" I said to her.

"Before I answer you, I have questions of my own," she said.

"Why are you here? Did you do something to him too? If no is your answer, I guess you're lost in these woods, and you're trying to find your way home like the others?" she said.

"The others? What are you talking about?" I asked her.

"There's nothing to worry about, Corey, for right now, I should say," Sage said to me.

"Well, anyway, to answer your questions, I don't know why I'm here. I know I didn't do anything to the old man, but he feels I did and I am lost. I just want to get out of here. Can you help me?"

"Yes, I can. The real question is do I want to help you?" she said to me.

I stood quiet, trying to figure out why she wouldn't help me.

"Are you there?" she asked.

"Yes, Sage," I answered, and then she began speaking again.

"Did you meet Mr. Stevens's son?" Sage asked.

"Yes," I told her.

"Did he like you?" she asked.

"What? Why are you asking me that? I don't know, Sage," I said to her.

"Did he try to help you?" she asked me.

"Yes, and what is with these questions about his son?" I asked her.

"Bobby likes you; as long as he likes you, he will help you. Bobby is crazy but less crazy than his father, if that makes any sense to you."

"Yes, as crazy as it sounds," I said to her.

"Quiet! The dogs are coming! Hide!" she said to me.

I moved back and stood still while the dogs were walking around the barn. As I stood there, I could feel something dripping down on me. My heart was racing, but I knew I couldn't move. Whatever it was, it was constantly dripping down my forehead and it was burning my eyes. I could feel the dogs getting closer. *Stay still, no matter what,* I said to myself. Before I knew it, one of them was right in front of me. The dog began to bark, I could hear the other dog running toward me. I wanted to scream; instead, Sage blew a whistle and the dogs went crazy. "Get out of here!" she yelled. The dogs barked even more. Sage blew the whistle again, and the dogs ran out of the barn. I stood there crying, not knowing what was going to happen to me.

"Shut up," Sage yelled. "Pull yourself together. There's no time for you to lose it. Make up your mind. Do you want to live or die?"

"Live, of course," I said to her.

"So shut up," she said again.

I wiped my eyes and pulled myself together like she said.

"I need you to wipe what was dripping all around you now," she told me.

"Why am I to do this?" I asked her.

"To mask your scent from the dogs, and please don't ask what it is that you're rubbing on your body, because right now, it doesn't matter," she said to me.

I did everything Sage said, and then I sat next to the box.

"Now, I need you to listen to me," she said. "I have helped a few people to find their way before you came along. They promised to send help; as you can see, they didn't. Maybe they were killed? Who knows what happened? The only thing I do know is that you must make it up the hill. Corey, the only way you will make it up the hill is if you follow my instructions. Once you're free, you leave here and never come back. Don't go to the police. You act like this never happened. Do you understand?" Sage asked me.

"Yes!" I yelled. "Please get me out of here!" I said to her.

"No need to yell. I would like to help you, but I want to be set free first," she said.

"You can come with me," I told her.

"I wish I could, but I'm dying," Sage said to me.

"What? You're dying?"

"Yes, but don't worry," Sage said, and then she began asking me about the days of the week.

"What is today? I hope today is not Friday. He said he'll be back on Friday to finish me off."

"No, today is Monday," I told her, and then she began to cough. "Are you okay?"

"Yes, I'm fine, just tired; that's all," Sage said. "Now that I know what day it is, you have plenty of time to talk with me, and that would be so nice, don't you think?"

I didn't answer her right away; Sage was beginning to scare me. Why would she want to keep me here with her and not help me get out of here? Sage began to cough again. "Are you okay?" I asked.

This time, there was a long pause. "Yes, Corey, I already told you I'm just tired; that's all," she said in a low voice. I didn't want her to die before she told me how to get out of there. Was I selfish to only be thinking about myself? I hope not. I called Sage's name three times before she answered.

"Yes, Corey," she answered.

"I just want to find a way out of here, Sage. Can you help me?" I asked her.

"Yes, but not tonight. They are out there waiting for you in the woods."

"What did I do, Sage?" I asked her.

"Nothing at all," she said to me. "You just showed up at the wrong time, like me."

"I don't understand," I said to her.

"Quiet and just allow me to talk," Sage said.

I shut my mouth and began to listen. This is what Sage had to say.

"I took a shortcut home from school, so I wouldn't run into the problem children on the main road. As I ran through the field, I wanted to see if I could catch a butterfly with my hands. As I was running, I tripped over some books that were lying on the ground; I stood up and brushed myself off. While doing so, I noticed that they were the same books that I used for school. I picked them up and put them inside my book bag. When I go to school the next day, I would hand them in, hoping whoever lost them would be able to get them back. The more I walked, the more interesting my journey became. I noticed a shoe and a uniform shirt lying near the bushes. Walking down this path began to scare me. Who would leave their shoes and shirt behind and not notice? The books I could understand; it could have fallen out of their book bag if they were playing, but a shoe and a shirt? That would be very noticeable. Even though I had my concerns, I still chose to walk down the path—stupid, I know.

"The more I walked the more items I found. There was a sock and pair of panties lying next to a wallet. I picked up every item and put them inside my book bag, except the wallet. I looked inside; there was a picture of a family of five, a man, a woman, two little boys, and a young girl. *This must be the little girl's wallet and items I found.* Her face looked so innocent. *Maybe she's in trouble, and I need to help her. No, I need to get help for her. What happens if she needs help right away? What to do? What should I do? Damn it, I'm scared.* Before I could make up my mind, I heard a scream. I ducked down low and watched through the bushes. It was the girl, the same girl who was in the picture. She ran from out of the barn that was down the hill. 'Run, run,' I said to myself. But she stopped running and ducked low, behind a car. 'Why did you stop? No, don't stop. You can be found behind there!' I said to myself.

"A tall white man came out of the barn. He began looking under and behind everything that was in his sight. But he couldn't find her. Maybe she had done the right thing. He went back inside, and she took off running in my direction. A few seconds later, he came back outside. For a moment, he stood there and watched her run before blowing his whistle. I stood silent, because I did not want anyone to know I was there. I wanted her to get away, but why did she have to run in my direction. Before I knew it, two big dogs came running out of the barn. She looked back and saw them as well and began to scream. She ran in the opposite direction and made it halfway up the hill before one of the dogs jumped on her back. The other dog took ahold of her legs. She tried to fight, but there was no way she could win against those dogs. They dragged her body down the hill and then stopped a few feet in front of me. The dogs began to tear her body apart. With every bite, her body jumped, and when it did, I moved back. I tried to keep my distance, but somehow, I pressed down on a stick. I could hear one of the dogs barking and running through the field. 'Who's in those fucking bushes?' he yelled.

"I took off running as fast as I could. I never looked back. I made it to the top of the hill.

"As I took the next step, I tripped over a rock, which caused me to fall. My head hit the pavement. At the same time, the rest of my body landed on a bottle. People began walking toward me, asking a bunch of questions instead of helping me. One stranger asked if I was okay. While another asked, 'What is your name? What are you doing in that neck of the woods? Who do you belong to, child?' I never had the chance to answer; I was in so much pain. I tried to lift myself up, as I turned my head. The tall white man walked up.

"'Oh, I know who she belongs to,' he said and began to pick me up.

"'No, don't let him take me!' I said, as I was trying my best to push him off. Then I noticed blood. Was it my blood or blood from the young girl?

"'Are you sure you know her?' another stranger said to him.

"'Yes, let me take her to her parents before they begin to worry,' he said to them.

"'I don't know about that, sir. I need for you to put her down and wait for help to come before moving her. She's bleeding a lot.'

"'Yeah!' others in the crowd shouted.

"He placed me down and whispered, 'It's not over.'

"'No, don't let him go,' I said.

"'Why not, child? Speak up!' someone in the crowd shouted.

"I tried, but it was hard for me to breathe, and then my body began to shake."

"I don't want to hear anymore. Who are these people? I have to get out of here!" I said to Sage.

"Calm down, Corey," she said.

"Why? Why should I?" I asked her.

"Because I'm here," he said.

The next thing I knew, I was lying on the ground and could hear Sage screaming, "You leave her alone," and then I was hit with a shovel.

*   *   *

"Pause the tape, Joe," Peter said to me.

I was busy writing down details. I didn't notice that the Spirit of Murder was walking away.

"You can't leave! You haven't finished. What am I supposed to do with this?" I asked.

"Joe, I will be back; you will see me again. You have all the information that is needed. Use it and find out what happened to me. Look for my aunt Bessie. She will be able to tell you more," the spirit said.

"How will I find her? What am I supposed to say to her when I do?" I asked.

"Peter will help. Isn't that right?" the spirit said to Peter.

Peter never answered.

"I have one more question," I said.

"Go, but hurry."

"The body you took over belongs to a girl named Corey. What did she do for you to have the right to enter?" I asked.

"That's something that Peter will be able to tell you about. Ask him to tell you about the curse. I will see you again, and then we will be able to talk more. I have a body to enter," the spirit said to me as it walked into darkness.

"Come, Joe; gather your things, and let's go. We have Suzie's family to visit," Peter said.

"I'm scared, Peter. What am I to say?" I asked him.

"When you get there, God will give you the words to say," Peter said to me.

I just looked at him and then said, "I hope you're right about your God."

"My God? He's your God too," Peter said to me.

"My God, that sounds funny, but I do want to know more about him," I said to Peter.

"You will," Peter said to me.

"I'm ready," I said. "Wait, Dave; let's go."

Dave appeared in front of us. "I can't go, Joe; I must stay here and guard."

"Guard what?" I asked him.

"When you come back, then I will show you," he said to me.

"I have to come back here, Peter?" I asked.

Peter never answered me.

"Dave, you can go," Peter said to him. Dave walked into the light.

"Now, we can go," Peter said to me.

"Yes, but I would like to know what the Spirit of Murder was trying to tell me about Corey and the curse," I said to him.

"I will answer your questions, but we must walk and talk."

I wanted to rest, but I knew we had to move on. Not knowing what would be waiting for us outside those doors scared me.

"Joe, did you hear me?" Peter asked.

"Yes, let's walk and talk," I said to him.

"Joe, let me say it this way so you can understand. The sins of the mother and father shall be passed on to their children."

"Sins, what is that?" I asked him.

"Where is the book that Ms. Annabelle gave you?"

I stopped and opened my book bag. I took out the three books and showed him. He grabbed the brown book and said, "This one here is all that you need. It holds all the answers to your questions."

"This book," I said to him.

"Yes," he said.

"Now, we are going to find a place to eat and sleep; our God has prepared a place for us. Let's go."

We walked out the back door onto this narrow path. It was so dark and cold.

"Where are we?" I asked Peter.

"Quiet," he said to me.

As we walked, light was given so we could see each step. For some reason, I felt that there was something waiting for us in the darkness. The longer we walked, the colder it became. I could hear them making noise. I grabbed ahold of Peter's hand. "Joe!" the voice called.

"Don't listen to it," Peter said to me.

"Joe!" it called again, but this time, I saw the face of my brother.

"James!" I called, and then it disappeared. "James!" I yelled again.

"Joe, that is not your brother. Come on!" he said to me. Peter grabbed a tight hold of me, and I fought him the rest of the way.

"I'm hurting, Peter. I miss my brother James so much," I said to him.

"I know you do, Joe, and the devil knows it too," he said to me.

"I don't know what to do or what to think," I said.

"In life, Joe, there's a process that you have to go through in order for God to get you where you need to be."

"I just want the pain to stop. Can God stop the pain?" I asked him.

"Yes, God is able to do all things. Nothing is too big or too small for God," Peter said.

Before I knew it, a cabin was in front of us.

"Where did this come from? Are we still in Oak Steel?" I asked him.

"Yes, Joe," he said to me.

"I have never been to these places that you have taken me."

"The things you see, you can only see with your spiritual eyes," Peter said.

Spiritual eyes? I said to myself. I wanted to ask him what he meant by that, but I didn't. I was so tired and hungry I just wanted to rest. So as we walked in, the people inside rushed to Peter and sat him down quickly. I stood there and watched how they took care of him. Some brought him a change of clothing while others washed his feet. I wondered why the people were taking such good care of Peter. He was not God. Why would he be given such good treatment? They were dancing and singing. Not having the answer, I began to look around.

The ceilings were very high. A natural man wouldn't be able to change the lightbulbs. Wait; there were none. Where was this light coming from? It was so bright, beautiful, and strange at the same time. The walls were gold—not painted gold, actually made of gold itself. What was this handwriting all over the ceiling, windows, walls, and floors? Even though I couldn't understand the handwriting, I knew it must be very important. The way these people looked, I wondered how they could have such riches. I wanted to see more, but there was a gate blocking the entrance, preventing people from going further. I stood there, trying to figure out how I would be able to get through. Then he touched me. I jumped and then turned around.

"What are you doing?" he asked me.

"I was just looking around; that's all," I told him.

"Who are you with? I haven't seen you here before?" he said to me.

"I'm with Peter," I replied in a low voice.

"Why didn't you say so?" he said and then opened the gate.

I began to walk in, and then Peter called my name. I tried to pretend I didn't hear him. But this time, he called my name so loud that the dancing and the singing had stop.

"Joe, you're not ready for the things that are on the other side," Peter said to me.

I turned around and sat at the other side of the table far away from Peter.

"Joe, are you mad at me?" he asked.

I didn't answer him.

"I know you can hear me, and I know things seem unfair to you right now, but there are things that you are not ready for, even if you think you are," he said to me.

"I'm not ready to see what's behind the gate, but I'm ready to fight demons and talk to spirits? I'd rather have what's behind the gate," I retorted.

He laughed and then said, "You are in training, Joe; that's why I'm here. There will come a time when you will have to prove that you are able to go to the next level, so while you're in training, take your time and pay attention. You don't want to repeat the test," Peter said.

"There are so many rules. What happens if I mess up?" I asked Peter.

"You will make mistakes, Joe; that's why you're in training. This is where the mistakes should be made. God is always with you, and he always gives you the chance to fix things between you and him, yourself, and others, but you have to want to change and do things God's way," he said.

"His ways seems so hard," I said.

"People make things hard when they try to go against God. You will never be able to beat him. So why not do things his way? It will save you a lot of trouble and heartache," Peter said.

"The only thing I can do, Peter, is try," I told him.

"That's all he asks of you, that you try your best and give your all to him."

"But I'm still scared, Peter. I'm worried about what I will see next, and those things are not pretty," I said to him.

Peter laughed again and said, "God knows you are, but you can ask him to remove the fear from your heart."

"How do I speak to him? Is there a special place I should go?" I asked him.

"Joe, God hears us now."

"Really, Peter, I don't know what to say to God."

"Just talk to him like you and I are speaking," Peter said.

"Should I tell him my name so he will know who I am?" I asked.

"He knows who you are. God knows everything about you."

"Really?"

"Joe, stop stalling and talk to God," he said.

"God, I don't know what to say to you and I know you're busy. I just want to know if you will help me. Because I'm scared. I need your help. Thank you. How did I do?" I asked.

Before Peter could answer, I heard a voice speak to me. I jumped and began to look around.

"What is wrong, Joe?" Peter asked.

"Did you hear a voice?" I asked.

"No, what did it say, Joe?" he asked me.

"It said, 'What do you want me to help you with?'"

"So answer God, Joe," Peter said.

"I want you to help me make it to the end of this journey," I said out loud, and then I waited. I didn't hear anything else from God.

"What is wrong now?" Peter asked me.

"I told God what I wanted, but he didn't answer me. Do you think he heard me?"

"Yes, he did. Now you must believe that God will you help you and keep the faith no matter what may come your way," he said to me.

"What do you mean when you say, no matter what may come my way? I have a feeling that there's more I will have to go through. Am I correct?" I asked him.

"You're right," Peter said to me.

"Food, please," Peter called out. They rushed over with the food, and we began to eat.

"No," Peter said as he knocked the food out of my hand.

"What? Did I do something wrong?" I asked him.

"Yes, we must pray over everything we drink and eat," Peter said to me.

"Why is that?" I asked him.

"Can I show her, Father?" Peter asked.

"Keep your eyes on my plate," he said to me, and then he began praying. I saw bugs and something white and black being removed from the food.

"What were those bugs?" I asked.

"What you just saw gives you the answers on why you must pray on all things you eat and drink, Joe."

"You are so right. Now I'm going to pray over what I eat and drink," I said to Peter.

The next morning, I woke up to an empty house. "Where is everyone?" I said to myself.

"Peter!" I called, but there was no answer. I ate the rest of the food that was on the table. As I was eating, I looked to my left and saw that the gate was open. I got up from the table and walked over to the door. "Hello?" I said out loud, but there was no answer. I turned around, and there was the old man, the same man who was in the woods when I was bitten. I ran back to the table and sat down.

"Do you want to go inside?" he asked.

"No," I said to him.

"Yes, you do," he said.

"I'm not supposed to go in there," I said.

"Who told you that? Please don't say Peter," he said.

"Yes, Peter is the one," I replied.

"He's a liar; he doesn't want you to have the things that your God has for you. He wants to keep it all to himself," the man said to me.

"No, I don't think that is right," I said.

"So why won't he allow you to go inside?" he challenged.

"I will be able to go inside, but not right now. God wants me to wait; I think I will do that."

"You're willing to wait and not know what you're waiting for? Don't be so stupid."

"It might seem that way to you, but why should I trust you when you sent your dog to kill me?"

"That wasn't me," he said quickly.

"I think you should go, before Peter comes back," I told him.

"Peter is not the ruler over me," he said.

"That's what you say, but we both know he is well connected to God."

The old man lifted up the table and threw it across the room. I got up and stood in the corner.

"I control this and everything in it," he said and then threw another table across the room.

I didn't want to make him mad. I didn't know what to do right then. "Call on Jesus," a voice said to me.

"Jesus, help me, please!" The more I called on Jesus, the angrier he became. "It's not working," I said to the voice.

"Keep calling his name," the voice said to me.

The old man picked up two tables and threw them at me. I saw the tables coming right at me. I yelled, "Jesus, please help me," and then I closed my eyes. I felt a wind rush in front of me. I opened my eyes hoping to see Peter, and there she was, holding the tables in her hands. She gently placed them down on the floor.

"What took you so long?" he said to her.

She stood there and never answered him. "Grab your things, Joe, and let's go," she said to me.

"My book bag is gone," I said to her.

"Where is it?" she said to him.

"How should I know?" he said.

She began to walk over to him.

"Okay, stay there. No need to get physical. The bag is right next to her," he said to her.

I looked down, and there it was right by my feet. I put it on, and we walked right past him.

"Joe, we will meet again," he said.

I kept my eyes on him until he was out of my sight. She was walking too fast.

"Can we slow down?" I asked her.

"No," she answered.

"Why not?" I asked.

"They are looking for you now," she said.

"Who is looking for me?" I asked.

"The town, they know that you have the books," she told me.

"How do they know?" I asked.

"That doesn't matter; they do. We must get you to the house of the first victim, before they get there."

"Where is Peter?" I asked her.

"Around," she said.

"Can I see him?" I asked.

"No, I oversee this part," she said.

"Oversee? What are you talking about?" I said.

"I am the angel who oversees babies and children," she said to me.

"Where are your wings?" I asked.

"Did you ask the same question to Peter?" she asked.

"No," I said to her.

"So why do you ask the question now?"

"I never thought a woman could be an angel. Where I come from, women are treated like dirt. We are not allowed to have a powerful position," I said to her.

"Man's ways are not God's ways," she said.

"What is your name?" I asked her.

"My name is Tay'Lin, but you call me Lin," she said.

"How much longer do we have to walk?" I asked her.

"We are here," she said.

"Okay, now what do I do?" I asked.

"You tell them what she told you," she said to me.

"What happens if they don't believe me?" I said to her.

"They will, Joe."

We walked up to the gate; the house was huge. "Suzie comes from a rich family. Why would she want to kill herself?" I asked Lin.

"No more questions, Joe. Press the bell."

I was so scared that I paused for a moment.

"Joe . . ."

"Okay, don't be so pushy," I said to her. I pressed the bell and then waited.

"Yes, how may we help you?" a man's voice said.

"My name is . . ." and then I stopped. "Do I tell them my real name?" I asked Lin.

Lin just looked at me.

"Yes, how may we help you?" he asked again.

"My name is Joe, and I have some information about Suzie," I said. There was a brief moment of silence, and then the gate opened. There was a long path leading to the front of the house. As I walked down the path, my stomach began to bother me.

"I don't think I can do this," I said to Lin.

"Why not?" she asked.

"My stomach hurts," I said.

"Do you give me permission to touch you?" she asked.

"Yes," I said to her. "It really hurts."

I fell down to my knees. Lin went underneath my shirt and placed her hand on my stomach. I could feel her hand becoming hot, and then there was a pull. After the pull, I threw up. Lin helped me to my feet.

"What was wrong with me?" I asked her.

"You ate that food without praying first," she said.

"It was the same plate of food that I ate from before I went to sleep," I said.

"Was it?"

I couldn't say anything else. She was right. I had to be more careful and aware of my surroundings. We continued walking, and you could see the horses and cows on the land. The house was so beautiful. I was amazed by what I saw. Lin called my name. "Joe! Pay attention.

Don't let the natural things fool you. You must look forward; don't worry about what's going on behind you or what is happening on the side of you. God is in the future, not in your past."

I didn't fully understand what she was trying to tell me, but I knew I would get it before this trip was over.

Before we could reach the top step, a woman came to the door.

"I was told you had some information about my daughter Suzie," she said to me.

"Yes."

"How could that be? You wouldn't have known her. She's been dead over fifteen years; you can't be any older than twelve years old," she said.

I looked over to Lin, hoping she would help me.

"I never met her while she was living," I said to her.

"You're trying to tell me that the dead talk to you?" she said to me.

"Yes, in this situation," I said.

"I don't have time for this foolishness. Why did you come here?"

"If you just give me a chance, I can tell you what happened to her, and it's not what the news reports or the police made it out to be. I will be able to give you some closure if you allow me," I said.

She stood there for a moment and then began to cry.

"For years, I wondered why she would just kill herself and the family; that wasn't like her. I wanted to know what pushed her to that point. I blamed myself, and so did her father," she said.

"I have the answers to your questions, if you'll just allow me to share them with you," I said.

She wiped her face and then said, "You have fifteen minutes. Come around the back. I will meet you there." When I walked around, Suzie was standing there with two men beside her, one on each side. She smiled at me. Suzie's mother came out and sat at the table. She told me to sit with her.

"A young girl travels all this way, you must have something important to tell me."

"If I was to tell you that Suzie is here with us, would you believe me?" I asked her.

"Do you see her?" she asked.

"Yes," I told her.

"Can she hear us?" she asked me.

"Yes," I replied.

Suzie touched her hand.

"I can feel something touching my hand," she said.

"That's Suzie," I said to her.

"I miss you so much! I just wish you would have talked to me," she said to her. "Why did she kill herself?" She turned to me.

"Suzie walked in on her husband and son having sex," I said.

"No, that can't be true," she protested.

"It is," I confirmed.

I took out my book and read my notes to her.

"She has been through so much, and I saw the signs. I wish I would have gotten her some help sooner," she said.

"You're not the one to blame," I assured her.

"Can you tell me what she is wearing?" she asked.

Before I could tell her, she answered her own question. "A blue dress, is that correct?"

"Yes," I said to her.

"I have to go, Joe," Suzie said to me.

"She has to go," I said to Suzie's mother.

"I understand. I love you, Suzie!" she said.

Suzie stood up, and both men grabbed her by the arms. They walked her away.

"Is she gone?" she asked.

"Yes, she left," I said.

"Thank you, Joe, so now where are you off to?"

"I must go and continue on with my journey," I said.

"You go around letting the victim's loved ones know what happened to them?" she asked.

"There's more to it than that," I said.

"Where is your family?" she asked me.

"My family wasn't allowed to come."

"Is there a God?" she asked.

I stared at her before answering. "Yes, there is a God."

"I knew it, I don't know how, but I did. Before you go, I have something to give you. Please wait," she said. She went inside and came back out with a book and a folded paper bag. "Take this." She handed it to me.

"Thank you," I said to her. "I really do have to go. I'm sorry, you never told me your name."

"Mrs. Hennery, you can call me."

"Thank you once again, Mrs. Hennery." I packed up my things, and we ran into the woods.

"Something is following us," Lin said to me. I began to look around as well.

"Show yourself!" she said, and it did.

"Oh, I am so sorry; I didn't mean to scare you. I don't know where I am. I was trying to find my way home, but every time I do, I run into these things in the woods," she said.

"What do you want?" Lin asked.

"I don't know. I was told that I needed to find a young girl named Joe, and she would be able to help me. Are you Joe?" she asked me.

"Yes, I am," I told her.

"Am I dead?" she asked me.

I just stood there and didn't answer. By the woman's skin, it looked like someone had set her on fire. She was very hard to look at. I tried not to focus too much on how she looked, but it was difficult.

"I take the silence as a yes?" she said.

"What happened to you?" I asked her.

"My husband and my stepson is what happened to me," she said in a loud voice.

"What did they do?" I asked.

"Where are my kids? I know they're dead. Where are they?" she yelled.

"I can't help you when you're like this; you have to calm down."

She looked at me and then at Lin. "Are you dead too?" she asked Lin.

"You didn't come here for me; she is the one who can help you, but only if you want her help. If not, we have to move on," Lin told her.

"I don't know what to do. One minute, I am alive, and the next thing I know, I'm dead," she said.

"I don't think you're ready to tell me your story. I have to go," I said.

"Why not?" a voice said to me from behind the bushes. I turned in that direction.

"Show yourself to me," I said to the voice.

As soon as I said that, they all came out of the bushes and began walking toward me.

"Stop right there!" I ordered them.

"Are they all here to see me?" I asked Lin.

"Yes, Joe," she said.

"How am I going to be able to help all of them? There're too many," I said to her.

"God gave you this journey, because he knew you would be able to finish it. Remember, God will never give you more than you can handle," Lin replied.

"I hope you're right," I said. Then I turned back to them.

"I can only help one at a time. I need you to go back where you came from and wait. Only she can stay, because she was here first," I said to them.

"Why is that?" a young man said to me from the crowd. "We all have the right to have our story told. What makes her so special?"

The crowd began to get angry, and they all approached me.

"What do I do?" I asked Lin.

"God gave you the power and the authority; they must obey your command," she said.

"Stop in the name of Jesus, and go back to where you came from," I said. They stopped and began to walk back into the woods. *I cannot believe that they listened to me!* I said to myself.

"Joe, I want you to understand it's not you who holds the power. It's power in the name of Jesus; he dwells in you, because of that, you are able to do anything through Jesus Christ, who strengthens you."

How could she have known what I was thinking? This journey was getting more interesting. I bent down, took off my book bag, and pulled out the book the woman had written in to see if I could locate her story.

"What is your name?" I asked her.

"My name is Mary Jane Smith," she said.

I went down the list, and her name was at the very end. "I wasn't supposed to see you yet," I said to her.

"Why not? I'm here," she said.

"I have to follow the instructions that were given to me," I said.

"So what am I supposed to do? Just sit and wait for my time to come?" she said.

"Yes, I'm sorry, but I can't take your story right now," I said.

"I understand," she said to me. I put the book back in my bag, and then she stood.

"You will help me?" she said and grabbed my wrist.

Lin pushed her, and she flew into the bushes.

"Let's go, Joe," Lin said to me.

Mary Jane Smith came out of the bushes and began to scream. These tall creatures came out of the woods and from underneath the ground.

"We won't make it to our next stop; there're too many of them," I said to myself, but we kept running. "Lin, maybe I should let her tell her story," I said.

"You never make a deal with the devil. You always do what God tells you, Joe," she said.

"Lin, they are coming," I said.

Lin stopped and said, "Let them come; for some reason, you think the evil has more power than God, and that's not true. I run because you are scared. That fear will cause you to get hurt," she said.

"They are coming, Lin. Don't you see them?" I said.

"Yes, I do, Joe, and I am not scared. You shouldn't be either."

They were about six feet away from us, and then she said, "Father, in the name of Jesus, shield us and cloak us from the enemy." This bubble came over us. The creatures stopped, and they began looking around, as if they couldn't see us.

"They can't see us, Lin!" I said.

"I know that, Joe."

We walked right through them. I couldn't believe it. "How is this happening?" I asked.

"Enough! Stop looking back. Keep your eyes forward," she said to me. "Where did you go wrong with Mary Jane Smith?"

"I don't know what you're talking about," I said.

"You never take your eyes off them, and you did with her," she clarified.

"I knew you were there and nothing would happen to me," I said.

"I and the others won't always be around as much as we are now. You must pay attention to what we say and do. Joe, you will be able to do what we do and more. There will be a test after every journey before you get to the next one. It's up to you if you want to pass or repeat the test," Lin said.

"I'm trying; it's so much to process at one time," I told her.

"Joe, stop making excuses," she said.

"I don't want to talk anymore," I said.

"Why? Because I'm not telling you what you want to hear?"

"No, that's not it. It's just a lot for me. You don't understand."

"We are almost at our rest stop. You should eat and rest; we have a long night ahead of us. I will be back to get you," Lin said.

"Where are you going?" I asked her.

"Back to my father to gather more strength and to get my next assignment."

"Does God supply all of your needs?" I asked her.

"Yes, Joe. Just ask in the name of Jesus for the things that you want."

"And I will get it? Everything that I ask for?" I asked.

"Not in that way. Sometimes, we ask for things that we don't need. God gives us what we need and more. There will be times you may ask God for something and he might not give it to you, for a lot of reasons, like it may be harmful to you, God may have something better for you, or you may not be ready for the things that you are asking for," she explained.

"I understand," I said.

"I will see you in the morning. Don't leave until I come," Lin said.

I couldn't wait to go inside so I could get the special treatment they gave Peter. I walked inside this hidden house, and all eyes were on me. It was dirty, and the people in there were dirty too. I didn't want to sleep there or have anything to eat from there. I quickly turned around to leave.

"Can I help you?" the old man asked.

"No, I was just leaving," I said.

"No, you don't want to go out there. It won't be safe for you," he said.

"I don't think I belong here," I said.

"Why not? Is it because you think you're better than us?" he asked me.

"No, that's not it," I said.

"So what is it then?" he asked me.

"I don't know, but I have to go," I said.

"You shouldn't judge people by their outside appearance. You should judge them by their fruits and what's inside of their hearts. You can go. I won't force you to stay. What you're looking for is right across the street, but it's not what you need," he said and then moved from in front of the door.

"I don't know what he's talking about," I said to myself.

I walked across the street. The place was much cleaner, and the people seemed to be people of wealth. I sat down and waited for them to bring some food like they had done for Peter, but no one ever came. So I just sat there wondering what I was going to do. Three women walked over to me.

"How may we help you?" one of them said.

"I would like to have something to eat, please," I said.

"This little girl would like to have something to eat," the second woman said.

"What the hell do you want to eat, little bitch?" the third woman said to me.

"I just want something to eat; that's all," I said.

"What is your name?" they asked me.

"Joe," I told them.

"Does anyone know Joe?" the third woman yelled out.

"We don't know anyone by that name," a few of the crowd members said.

"Why are you here?" she asked me.

"I'm a friend of Peter's," I said.

"Peter Long?" they asked me.

"Yes," I said to them.

"Where is he? Who has he come for?" the first woman said. Then she began looking around.

"No, he's not with me," I said to them.

"Do you know who we are and what we do?" she asked.

"No, I don't. I came here because I didn't want to be with those across the street," I said.

"So you have chosen to come to this side?" she said to me.

"This side? What are you talking about?" I said.

"She doesn't know. Lack of knowledge will be the cause of death. Bring her some food right away!" The women left my table.

I was brought more than enough food. I prayed over my food like I was told. As soon as I started to take a bite of the bread, Peter smacked it out of my hand.

"Peter!" everyone said as they ran for cover.

"Up, get up now!" he ordered. He grabbed my arm and pushed me out of the door.

"What are you doing in here?" he asked.

"I didn't like where Lin brought me," I said.

"You don't make the decision, Joe. God makes all of the rules," he said.

"What rule did I break, Peter?" I asked him.

"God placed you where he wanted you to be, but you had to have things your way," he said.

"It's too much for me. Why don't you get that?" I said.

"What's too much? God is here with you. He has sent us to help you, but you won't listen, and you won't take the time out to read the book."

"I think God made a mistake. I'm not the one for this. I'm only twelve. I should be playing with kids my own age, not dealing with spirits, demons, or whatever else that may come my way. It's hard for me to process this, Peter. It may have been easy for you, but it's not for me."

"Your tears will not change the plans that God has for you. We all have been through something, some worse than others, but the more you go against God, the worse things will become," he said.

"Leave her alone. Why are you trying to force your beliefs on her?" the old man with the dog said to Peter.

"Shut your mouth," Peter said.

"Oh. Peter, you know better than this; you are in my home. She came to us, and you know the rules. She has the free will to choose. Isn't that right?" the man with the dog said to Peter.

"Joe, don't listen to him," Peter said.

"Joe, on this side, we don't have rules. We do what we want and how we want to do it. The only thing God wants to do is control you and make you do things his way. If you come with me, I will allow you to do what you like. Is that what you want, Joe?" he said to me and then held out his hand.

I stood there looking at Peter's face.

"No, I will finish with God. I know you're a liar," I said to him.

"You fool! The next time, I will make sure that you die!" Then he walked inside the house.

I could still tell that Peter was very angry with me. As soon as we walked inside the other house, he said to them, "Who let her leave? Answer me!" he yelled.

The old man walked up and said, "Peter, you know we can't make her stay against her will. She has the right to choose, and she chose not to stay."

"She needs food and water right now," Peter said to them.

As we began to sit, Lin showed up.

"What are you doing here?" Peter said.

"Our father needs to see you at once," she told him.

Peter hit the table and left.

"I hope I didn't get him into trouble," I said to Lin.

"No, this is between him and God. God is not pleased by what you did. You can't go around changing things because they don't feel good to you. That's not how it works, Joe. You have what you need in this bag of yours. Read the books Ms. Annabelle gave you and the notes that the woman before left behind. God gives us everything we need on our journeys, but it's up to us to use them," she said.

"I'm sorry, Lin," I said.

"No, you have to get things right with God, not with me," she said.

"How do I do that?" I asked her.

"By asking God to forgive you for all of your sins," she said to me.

"Right now, in front of everyone?"

"You are worried about what others think instead of being afraid of what God might do to you if you keep going against him?"

I got on my knees and asked God to forgive me.

"Did he forgive me?" I asked her.

"Yes, he did. Now you have to forgive yourself. Make sure you eat and get some rest. We will be leaving in a few hours," Lin said and walked away.

I finished eating and took out the book that the woman before had written in. I wanted to know more about Mary Jane Smith. What happened to her, and why was she so angry? *Here it is. It looks like she has already told her story from what I can tell from what is written. Maybe she doesn't recall telling her story. Maybe from what I'm reading, I'm not getting the full understanding of what's going on.* This is what was written about Mary Jane Smith.

Chapter Five

The Wooden Floor / The Notes

Even a child is known by his actions,
by whether his conduct is pure and right.
—Proverbs 20:11 (NKJV)

Train up a child in the way he should go:
and when he is old, he will not depart from it.
—Proverbs 22:6 (NKJV)

Discipline your son, and he will give you peace;
he will bring delight to your soul.
—Proverbs 29:17 (NKJV)

Hello, my name is Mary Jane Smith. I was born in Greensboro, North Carolina, to a young couple named Tim Simmons and Linda Anna Stone. I lived there until I was about twenty-one years old. The life with my parents was very stressful. They were so controlling and not easy to reason with. In their household, it was their way or no way, and I had to obey all the rules. What can one say to that? It was their house; if I didn't like how things were being run, I could just leave. That was what my father would tell me time after time. I could leave, but when I do go, I could never come back. However, I did have a major problem. I had nowhere to go and no clue where I would live. My job didn't pay enough for me to have my own place. I guessed I would be living there forever. Before I knew it, I fell in love with an older man named Sam Smith. No one in my family or town was thrilled about our relationship, like I really cared about what others had to say. Sam was forty-one and had a ten-year-old son named Richard. I was in love.

My mother disagreed with my decision, and every time she saw me, she always had something to say. These are my mother's very own words: "Mary Jane Simmons, what would a grown man want with a little girl and *my little girl* at that." I would just look at her and wait for her to finish speaking. "Mary, he only wants to control you, baby; that's all. He doesn't love you the way you think he does. What do you have to offer him? Nothing but what's between your legs. A relationship is more than that. After a while, he will get bored with you. Right now, you're his toy. You don't have a clue to what life is about. By him being older than you, he has more life experience than you. Please listen to me; I'm telling you what's best for you. I wouldn't tell you anything that would hurt you. Are you listening to me?" she would say afterward and then walk out of the room.

"She makes me sick," I would say to myself. Who would want to hear that the person she loved really didn't love her the same way? Even if it was the truth, I didn't want to hear that. It seemed to me that she always had something bad to say about him. Why couldn't she just let us be? I couldn't wait for us to get married.

The second year of marriage, Sam brought me to New York City. The lifestyle and the pace were very different from those of the South. It took me some time to get used to, but it was nothing like living at home. He bought us a house, which was located at 1622 Fountain Avenue. I've been there for over thirty years now. I raised my children and had to bury each and every one of them. My husband was the only one I had until two months ago when he passed as well. I'm so alone now; no one comes to visit me. I made my neighborhood my life. People call me the old bat who stays in the window. I see and hear it all. If you don't want your business known, don't put it out there. It's not what you do; it's how you do it. Watch the company that you keep. They might act like they are your friends, but deep down, they are not, and you will meet plenty of those through life experience itself.

I was a giver, always wanting to help others. In a way, it was a good thing. However, it might not be. There were people who preyed on my goodness for their own welfare, but I could spot them from far away. They only called and came by when they needed something. When I needed them, they were nowhere to be found or always had a story for why they couldn't help me. What could I do but shake my head and hope that they changed? There was no need to get upset, because I knew what to expect from the beginning. It hurt more when I was used by a family member. The old saying is "Your family would be the first one to do it to you." What about this one, "A stranger will treat you better than the ones you love." I always thought family was supposed to stick together no matter what. Do you agree with that part? No matter what? I knew there were some people who might feel differently. As for me, there were no limits when it came to my children. I would protect them to the bitter end. I know I'm not the only one who feels that way. For those who may disagree, that is your right. Oh, I'm sorry; I'm so busy preaching to you. Please forgive me because that's not the purpose of my story. Where was I? Can you help me remember? You know what? Don't worry about it; I can recall it all now. I was talking about my husband and me.

As I began living with Sam and his son, I noticed something right away. Richard was always angry, and Sam could not control him. Since Sam had no control, it made it even harder on me. Two adults in the household, but the child was running the show? How could that be? As time went on, things took a turn for the worse. Sam and I began to argue a lot. I could not say anything to him about his son, but that wasn't fair to the children that we had together. I treated everyone the same. There was no favoritism, but Sam did not see it that way. All the things he promised me and the life he said we would have, it was all a lie. It was all a plan to get me away from my family. Without my family being around, I would have to depend on him for everything. With me having to do that, he had control. Could I be wrong? Yes, but I know that I'm not. Actions speak louder than words in all situations.

When Richard was around, I had to keep a close watch as he played with his sisters and brothers. He played to hurt. When I would get involved with how he played with the children, Richard would give me this strange look. The look he gave me made me watch him even more, especially now that he was mad at me. I tried to reach out to him, but the more I tried, the more he closed up. What was one to do?

I'd been thinking about leaving Sam for some time. Sam always said I was able to leave anytime I got ready, but I couldn't take the children with me. Leaving my children behind was never an option. So I started working part-time behind Sam's back. I needed money so I could make it back home with the kids. A girlfriend of mine knew of my situation and offered me a job babysitting. Sam thought I was just hanging out at her house with the kids, but I was planning to escape.

Sam would make a big fuss about me being over at Ann's house. The things that he complained about were so stupid, if you ask me, but I knew he was trying to start a fight with me so I wouldn't go to her house. I was not about to allow that to happen. So I fixed everything he had a problem with, and still he wasn't happy. What was a girl to do?

I started cooking dinner earlier, just because I wanted everything to be done and ready for Sam when he got home. As I was getting the house in order one day, there was a knock on the door. It was a couple looking for their daughter Sara. She was last seen three days earlier with a couple of boys. They were wondering if my son was one of them. I called Richard to the door. By the look on his face and the answers that he gave, I could tell he knew more than what he was telling. I asked him again if he knew the girl or had ever seen her.

"No, I told you, I don't know any girl by that name. Can I go now?" he said.

I allowed him to remove himself, and then I told the couple that I was sorry and hoped they found their daughter soon. They just stood there looking at me. As I tried to close the door, the young man placed his hand in the way and said, "Is that it? I know you don't believe your son."

"I don't know what you mean," I said to him.

"He knows more than what he is telling. Let me talk to him," he said.

"No, I can't allow that, sir," I told him.

"My daughter is missing, ma'am. Do you understand that?" his wife yelled.

"Yes, but I can't allow you to question my son," I said to her.

"Your son would watch my daughter walk home from school every day," the man said.

"How do you know that?" I asked.

"She would tell us about your son always watching her. Sara was afraid of the things he would say to her in and out of school."

"Can you tell me what she said?" I asked.

"No, I won't!" he screamed. "They went to the same school. How is it that your son doesn't know who she is?" he asked me.

"Because they went to the same school that does not mean that they knew each other," I told him.

"Your son knows more than he is telling. We will be back."

Then he let go of the door. I slammed the door and yelled for Richard.

"Are they gone, Mother? What did you tell them?" he asked.

"What was I supposed to tell them, Richard? Have you seen that girl in your school before?" I asked him.

"Yes, I have," he said.

"So you do know her?" I replied.

"No, I don't know her. I see a lot of people in school. That doesn't mean that I know them," he stated.

"If you know anything, I want you to tell me," I said to him.

"A person should only know what they are able to handle," he said.

"I don't know what you mean by that statement, but when your father comes home, he will deal with you. Go to your room, and don't come out until he gets here," I told him.

Richard just looked at me and walked back upstairs. I began to make my way back to the kitchen to finish my dinner. Before I could put the chicken in the oven, there was a knock on the door. I opened the door. It was Sara's father again, asking for my husband.

"He's not home yet," I told him.

"I'll wait until he comes home," he said.

"You can wait outside for him if you like," I said to him, and then I started to close the door. He placed his body in the way and then pushed the door wide open.

"I will wait for him in here," and then he slammed the door behind him.

I backed up into the kitchen to grab the knife I had placed beside the cup that was on the table, but it wasn't there. He began to look around the house.

"I know he knows where my daughter is. Where is he?" he screamed.

I yelled for Richard to run and hide. Sara's father went into the girls' room.

"You have two little girls," he said to me.

"Leave them alone!" I yelled.

He began walking toward them. I jumped on his back, and we began to fight. He threw me off; my head hit the children's crib. I became dizzy, but I could hear the front door open. "Sam!" I yelled.

Sara's father walked toward the door to leave. Richard ran inside the room and rammed something into his stomach. Sara's father turned toward me, grabbed ahold of the knife, and collapsed. I stood there staring at his body. Richard grabbed his legs and then dragged his body out of the room. I followed him to see what he was doing. He dragged the body downstairs into the basement. He pulled back five pieces of the wooden floor and placed the body in there.

"What are you doing?" I asked as I walked toward him.

"You shouldn't be here, Mother," he said to me.

I could see there was another body in there.

"Is that Sara's body, Richard?" I asked.

"You're not supposed to be in here," he said to me again.

I ran up the stairs. Sam was standing by the door. "Sam, there are dead bodies in the basement, underneath the wooden floor," I told him.

"Calm down, Mary. I know all about it," he said.

"You know? I have to get out of here." I tried to get around him, but he grabbed me.

"Where do you think you're going, Mother?" Richard asked me.

"Mary, just sit down and listen to us," Sam said to me.

"Why should I? You're going to kill me too?" I asked.

"Just sit your ass down and listen!" Sam shouted.

"I can't see you, and I can't breathe!" I yelled out to Sam.

Sam sat me down on the steps and then walked over to Richard.

"What did you do to your mother?" he asked Richard.

"I put something in her drink," he answered.

"What was it? What did you give her?" Sam screamed.

"You don't need her. You have me!" he said.

"What did you give her?" he asked again.

"Get your hands off me. You're the doctor. Save your bitch!" he yelled.

Those were the last words I heard.

*   *   *

Peter yelled, "Joe!" I dropped the book and tried my best to hide it behind me. I knew what he was going to ask me, so I kept my head down the entire time he was speaking to me.

"What are you doing?" Peter asked me.

"I don't want to say," I said to him.

"I already know; I just want you to explain to me why," Peter said.

"Why what?" I asked.

"Why would you read the story about Mary Ann Smith when it wasn't her time for the story to be told?" he said to me.

I lifted my head and said nothing, because I knew he was right.

"Sometimes people make life worse than God intends it to be for them, just because they don't want to listen," Peter said to me.

"Does it change things?" I asked him.

"No, not at this moment. God knew you were going to do what you did. He knows everything. What you should have done with your time is read the book Ms. Annabelle gave you. The book will help you in so many ways," Peter said to me.

"I will read it, Peter," I said to him.

"Gather your things. We have another family to visit," he said.

I gathered my things. For some reason, I knew in my heart I had messed up. I just didn't feel right about what I'd done. I should have never gone ahead when I was told not to. *I hope God can forgive me again*, I said to myself.

"I'm ready, Peter," I said to him.

"Now you tell me who is next on the list," he said to me.

"I was supposed to visit the young teenager's family first. Instead, I paid Suzie's family a visit. I keep messing up. God has to be upset with me," I said to Peter.

"None of us is perfect, Joe. You will make mistakes, but you have to learn from them," he said to me.

"I don't see you messing up. You do everything right," I said.

"No, not I, but the Father who is in heaven is perfect. I made plenty of mistakes, Joe. I used to lie and steal when I was in the world, and I knew it was wrong. I felt the world owed me something, so I took what I thought was mine," Peter said.

"What did God do to you?" I asked him.

"I refused to do things his way like you. I had so many questions that needed to be answered by God before I would do anything he said for me to do. In one day, I lost it all: my wife left me, I lost my job, and my house burned down," he said.

"God did that to you?" I asked.

"No, I did it to myself. God gives us the will to choose. At that time, I had chosen the things of the world. I didn't realize it was God who gave me that job, it was God who bought me that house, and it was the Lord who allowed me to meet my wife. God had done so many things for me known and unknown, but I refused to do this one thing that God asked of me," Peter explained.

"What was it?" I asked of him.

"To honor the woman who gave birth to me. Do you believe I told him no? I was so angry at my mother, so angry at one point that I hated her for the things she had done to me. God understood my pain, but that still didn't give me the right to disrespect her. The word of God says, 'Honor your mother and father and your days on earth shall be prolonged.' God showed me how to love, honor, and respect my mother his way. If I couldn't forgive my mother, God wouldn't forgive me, and, Joe, I needed to be forgiven for the things I had said and done to people."

"Are you telling me that I have to forgive my mother, Peter?" I said to him.

"Yes, if you want God to forgive you," he said.

"My brother died because of her!" I yelled at him.

"I know that."

"If you know so much, why are you trying to make me do something that I do not want to do?" I asked him.

"Joe, if you don't forgive, you can't move on," Peter said.

"Why is that? He chose me for this. I was fine before he came along," I said to Peter.

"Were you fine, Joe?"

"I would have figured it all out on my own," I said.

"So that is what you will do," he said to me, as he walked away.

"I will do this work without you. Do you hear me?" I yelled. And then it became very cold.

I walked in the direction the book indicated. I saw a house not too far away from where I stood. I knocked on the door, and Lin opened it.

"Lin," I said, "please help me. I can't feel my toes."

Lin never answered me.

"Lin, please help me. Why are you acting like you don't know me? Lin, it's me Joe!"

"I have to close the door now," she said to me.

"Lin, don't close the door. Lin!" I yelled as the door slammed in my face. I walked across the street to the other house and knocked on the door. Dave opened the door.

"Dave, help me! Please let me in," I said.

"Joe, what did you do?" he said to me.

"What are you talking about?" I asked.

"We were given orders not to help you. I have to close the door now, Joe."

"You'd rather have me die instead of helping me?" I yelled out loud.

Then it began to snow. I walked away from the door, and there was the man with the dog. "Come; I will help you. Come with me."

"I will go with him if you don't help me!" I yelled.

The ground began to tremble, and then the tree branches began to move back and forth with a forceful wind. "I have other things I need to attend to. You're not a threat to me at this moment." The old man walked away. Lightning struck all around me. I ran into the woods. My legs gave out on me. I couldn't feel them.

I pulled myself up with my upper body, and then my arms became weak. I lay there on my back looking up toward the sky. I was cold and covered with snow. "Choose this day whom you may serve," a voice said to me. I looked around and saw Peter, Lin, and Dave standing around me. "Chose this day whom you may serve," the voice said to me again.

I began to cry, and then I yelled, "I choose you this day to serve, God."

Lin ran over to me and said, "Please, God, spare her life; she has chosen."

"No, I have my own petition." The man with the dog stepped out of the bushes.

"Carry her to the stone, and lay her there at once," the voice told Lin and Peter.

They laid me on the stone, and a huge bubble covered me. I couldn't hear anything else that was being said. I lay there until the next morning.

"Joe, get up," Peter said to me.

As I sat up, I realized I couldn't feel my legs. "What has happened to my legs, Peter?"

"We have to go," he said.

"Is this my punishment from God?" I asked him.

"I'm not allowed to speak to you about this," he said.

"How will I get around without the use of my legs?" I said.

"Are you saying you're willing to go on, even though you can't walk?" Peter said.

"Yes," I answered.

Peter placed me in a wheelchair, and we began our journey through the woods. "We need to get you something to eat," Peter said. We stopped at this little store to grab something to eat. As we were waiting for our food, my legs began to hurt.

"My legs are hurting me," I said to Peter.

"What time is it?" he asked the man sitting across from us.

"Six o'clock," he said to Peter.

"Peter, did you hear me? My legs are hurting. I need you to stop the pain. Touch my legs," I said to him.

"No, I can't, Joe," Peter said to me.

The pain started to increase. I grabbed his hand and placed it on my legs, but nothing happened. "Why can't you heal me like before?" I said.

Peter never answered me.

"I need to lie down, and I'm not hungry anymore," I said.

They placed me on some pillows, and I lay there in pain. As the hours passed, my legs began to turn black and blue.

"I'm in so much pain, Peter; I think I'm going to die."

Peter just stood there and didn't say a word.

The man with the dog appeared. He walked back and forth as he watched me in pain.

"God, please forgive me. Help me, Peter," I said to him.

Peter walked over to me and handed me the book out of my bag.

"Peter Long, you know the rules," the man with the dog said to him.

"No one ever mentioned I couldn't give her the book," Peter said.

"Just from that, she will die," the man with the dog said to Peter.

My legs felt like they were on fire. I screamed and screamed.

"Please, Peter, help me!"

Lin showed up.

"Lin, please help me," I said to her.

"Read the book. Everything you need is in the book," she said to me and then turned to a page that was about healing.

"She doesn't know how to use this book. I have nothing to be afraid of," the old man said.

The book was lying open to Isaiah, and this is what I read.

Isaiah 53:5

But He *was* wounded for our transgressions, *He was* bruised for our iniquities; The chastisement for our peace *was* upon Him, And by His stripes we are healed.

And then the pages turned to the book of Jeremiah.

Jeremiah 17:14

Heal me, Lord, and I will be healed; save me and I will be saved, for you are the one I praise.

Then the pages turned to Psalms.

Psalm 30:2

Lord my God, I called to you for help, and you healed me.

"Read it again, and this time, read it out loud," Lin said to me.

I read each passage three times. The more I read the words of God, the more pain I was in, but I didn't stop reading. I knew Peter had given this to me for a reason. I began praying and crying, reading God's words in between. Finally, at six o'clock in the morning, the pain was gone. I pulled back the covers, and my legs were back to their normal color.

Peter showed up and said, "How do you feel?"

"Tired and a little weak, but the pain has stopped. Thank you, Jesus."

"I'm surprised to hear that coming out of your mouth," he said.

"God was very upset with me, and he caused me to be in pain for twenty-four hours?"

"That's wasn't God, Joe. The devil put a petition against you—in other words, a request."

"What? I don't understand," I said to Peter.

"When God placed you in the bubble, the devil asked God to take away the use of your legs for one day and allow him to inflict pain upon you. The devil told God you would turn on him in that day. God granted him what he wanted, with some restrictions of course. That's why I could help you," Peter said to me.

"The man with the dog is the devil?" I asked.

"Yes, but there is more than just one," he said to me.

"So what will happen now?" I asked.

"We really do have to go. The devil is very angry that you got victory over him. From this day forth, he will do whatever he can to stop you from completing God's will," Peter said.

I got up and stumbled a little, but I was able to stand and walked out the door with Peter.

"We are on our way to visit another family," Peter said to me.

"I don't have enough information to visit another family right now. The spirits that I have met so far did not finish telling their stories," I said to Peter.

"The family that we are going to visit is yours," he said.

I just looked at him. I wasn't quite sure of what I would be walking into, but I knew I had to forgive my mother and my stepfather for what they had done to me and the death of my brother. I really needed God's help. I walked up to the door; before I could knock, my mother opened the door. She stared at me with tears in her eyes.

"Can I hug you?" she asked me.

"Yes," I told her.

"Do you want to come in?" she asked.

I paused for a moment because I was about to walk past where my brother was killed.

"I don't think I'm ready to come in right now. Maybe you should come outside so we can talk," I said to her.

"Please come in, Joe. Your sisters would love to see you. They will be home in a few minutes, and Steve won't be home for hours," my mother said.

I heard what she said, but I wasn't sure if I was ready.

"Please," she said, and I walked inside.

We sat at the kitchen table, and she just stared at me with tears flowing from her eyes.

"I'm so sorry, Joe, for what I have done and allowed to happen to you and your brother. Please forgive me. Will you forgive me?" she asked.

I wanted to tell her no, but I knew God wanted me to forgive her and I needed to for myself. Holding on to this hurt wasn't good for me. "I forgive you, Mother, but I just don't understand how you can still be with the man who killed your son," I said.

"I have to live with that pain, Joe, every day, and I know what he has done, but I love him," she said.

"You love him more than your own children," I said.

"I thought you came here to see how I was doing?" she said.

"I wonder, Mother, if you ever loved me," I said to her.

"I knew you would come back home; you're too young to make it on your own. Joe, you might not like my ways, but I am still your mother," she said.

"A mother," I said to her and stood up.

"No, Joe, don't go there with her. Stay focused," Peter said to me. I looked at him and sat back down.

"I don't know how you two covered up James's death, but God knows," I said to her.

"What? You want to judge me now, is that it?" my mother said.

"Me coming here, it wasn't for you; it was for me," I said to her.

"Yourself," she said.

"I needed to face the one who has hurt me and tell her that I love her and that I forgive her for everything she has done or even said to me. I pray to God, Mother, that he will help you become a better woman," I said to her.

"You pray to God for me? Is that what you just said? Fuck you and your God, you little bitch. You're one of them now. Get the hell out of my house and never come back here. Do you hear me, Joe? And if you do, I'll be forced to kill you myself," she said.

"May God bless you, Mother," I said to her, and I walked out of the house.

"Well, that didn't go too well," Peter said to me.

I just looked at him and started laughing. "I really don't know that woman anymore," I said to Peter.

"Sometimes, Joe, people will not have the same passion that you have or even want the same things that you want out of life, and that's okay. But you make sure you don't change just to please people. When you do that, you will never become the person God created you to be, because you want to be a people pleaser," Peter said.

"I hear what you are saying, but it still hurts, Peter. The only thing I wanted was for her just to love me, and that is the one thing she couldn't do," I said to him.

"I know it does, Joe, but you have to let it go. You can't make someone love you, you can't make someone be with you, and you can't make someone treat you right."

"I know what you are saying is true, but it still hurts, Peter." As we were walking, I noticed footprints appearing in front of us. "What is that?" I said out loud.

Peter stepped in front of me and said, "Stop. Be still." I stopped walking and stood still. I saw something run past very quickly.

"Oh, I saw something, Peter!" I said to him.

"Quiet, Joe!" he said to me. It ran behind me, and I screamed. "Joe," Peter said.

"Okay, okay," I said back. Whatever it was, it kept running around us. When it came around the fourth time, Peter swung his fist. Whatever it was flew into the gate of the house, and the gate broke. I knew my mother would come running out.

"Deal with your mother," Peter said to me.

I walked toward my mother. She was screaming and cursing at me.

"Why would you do this to the house?" she asked.

"I didn't do it," I said.

"Who did, Joe? You are the only one out here."

"You won't understand, Mother. You never believed me. There are other things living with us."

"No, there's not, Joe. You need help. I can't do this with you again."

"Again? What are you talking about?" I asked her.

"You would tell me about these monsters in your room. You were about three years old. The things that you would see, I wanted to believe you, but I never saw them for myself. I didn't know what to do. I was scared of you, Joe. Things would break in the house, and you would say the monsters done it. I knew you couldn't have done it, because you were too small. I just didn't understand why they were after my baby, whatever they were.

"The only ones who would speak about it were Ms. Annabelle and her husband. When they told me you were able to see things and what you were seeing, it was hard for me to believe. I told Steve, and he wasn't too thrilled."

"The things that I see are real, whether you believe it or not," I said.

"I had to make you think that it wasn't real, so you wouldn't tell anyone else. If this town had known about this, they would have killed us all. Those who do believe and want to help those who suffer from these demons or unclean spirits would be killed also. I wanted you to hate me so you would not want to come back here. There's nothing here for you, Joe. The demon that rules this town is powerful," she said to me.

"There is a God who is more powerful than these demons," I said to her.

"Yes, you're right, but this town doesn't pray and wants nothing to do with God. So the angels stand still and watch the devil destroy," my mother said to me.

"Joe, we have to leave now," Peter said to me.

"I need to go, Mother. I wish we had more time to talk. I love you," I said to her and then ran off.

"What happened? What was that thing, Peter?" I asked him.

"Less talking and more moving," he said.

"Turn right here," Peter said.

I turned, and there it stood. It was tall with a black covering all over its body. I screamed at the top of my lungs. Peter placed his hand over my mouth. "Quiet, Joe. I know it can't see you, but its ears are very sharp," Peter said. I shut my mouth and stood still. It moved back and forth trying to get a sense of where we were. But it couldn't pick anything up. Peter hit it with his fist, and it stumbled back and gave out a loud scream. "Duck down!" Peter said to me. It opened its mouth, threw a few black balls at us. One hit my foot and took ahold of my shoe. I kicked off my shoe and watched it cover my entire shoe and then it melted. I couldn't believe what I'd seen. Peter bent down and touched the dirt and then stood back. The ground began to bubble around this creature. "Move back," Peter said to me. The creature blew some black stuff out of its mouth once again and stopped the ground from bubbling. It began to laugh. When I saw that, I knew Peter and I were in trouble. This one wasn't like the rest. It was prepared to fight.

"Peter Long," it said out loud. "You know your tricks won't work on me. You act like we met yesterday."

"They sent you and not the leader," Peter said to it.

"It's protocol, Peter. You know the rules," it said.

I turned around, and Lin stood behind me.

"Where did you come from?" I asked her.

"No talking," she said to me. "The rules have changed," Lin said to it.

"By whose authority?" the creature asked.

"By the one who sent me, the one and only true and living God," Lin said.

"You send a woman to fight me? Is this the best that you can do?" it said loudly, looking up.

"Peter, you and Joe get out of here," Lin said to us.

Peter grabbed my hand, and we took off running. I could see them fighting and hear the creature as we ran through the woods. A man stood there with a cane in his hand. Right beside him, on each side, there were two giants. We stopped running and walked toward the man.

"I've been waiting for you for about three days now. You're way behind schedule," he said.

"There's been a lot going on. How may I help you?" I said.

"Joe, we might have to skip this one; they are coming!" Peter said to me.

The man heard what Peter said to me. "It's not my fault that you are behind. I have the right to tell my story like the rest of them. Who are you running from that you can't allow me to tell my side?" he asked me.

"I really don't know what they are, but they are not friendly," I said.

"Show yourself now," he said, and there were the faces of those who were trying to stop me from fulfilling God's will. "As of this moment, no one touches her until I finish my story. Do I make myself clear?" he said to them. They all started speaking in a language that I could not understand.

"Now that's settled; let us walk and talk," he said to us.

I took out my tape recorder and pressed PLAY.

"Who are these giants with you?" I asked him.

"They are angels here to make sure that I am kept here until judgment day," he said.

"So you already know where you're going?" I said.

"Yes, hell, I suppose," he said to me.

"How were you able to get those creatures to obey you? You are not God," I said.

"I am the one who rules on this side of town. Those are the weak ones; they are not stronger than I," he said.

"What is your name?" I asked him.

"My name is Richard, but my job is to deceive people," he said.

"Richard is your name. Hold on. Can we stop? It's hard for me to record, write, and walk at the same time," I said.

"We can sit at this table right here," Richard said.

I took out the book, and the name Richard was written nowhere. "We have a problem," I said.

"What is that?" he asked.

"Your name is not written in this book," I said.

"Richard is not in there? Try Bill."

I looked for the name Bill, and it was there. "How do I know this is you, since you have already lied to me?" I said.

"Ms. White had to leave a description of me," he said.

"Ms. White? Is that the name of the woman who had this job before me?" I asked.

"You didn't know. You don't know what happened to her?" he said.

"Peter Long, you didn't share with her what this journey entails," Bill said to Peter.

"Peter, what is he talking about? Is something going to happen to me?" I asked him.

"Joe, no one knows all of the details but God," he said.

"The things that you are telling me could be all lies," I said to Bill.

"It could be or maybe not. What would you do if you found out that Peter was the one lying to you? Do you really believe him?" he said to me.

"You don't know me," I said to Bill.

"Yes, yes, I do. I know more than you think," he said.

"Just tell me your story, so I can move on," I said.

"Ms. White is not dead; she is still alive. I just wanted you to know that before I begin my story," Bill said to me.

I didn't say anything to him or to Peter. What would be the use? I wouldn't be told what I wanted to know anyway.

"I'm ready to hear your story," I said.

"I've been waiting so long for my story to be told," he said to me.

He took off his hat. On top of his head sat these black things.

"I could put my hat back on if you want?" Bill said.

"What I need you to do is to tell your own story, Bill," I said.

He stood up and bumped into the two giants. "Give me room. I'm not going anywhere," he said.

"So she did write me in her book? What did she say?" he asked me.

"Maybe she did, and maybe she didn't," I said.

"You're learning," he said to me.

"Now tell me your story, Bill," I said.

When Bill started to speak, the air became cold.

"What's going on?" I asked.

"Just watch," Peter said to me.

A woman walked toward us, clapping her hands.

"Who is she, Bill?" I asked him.

"Yes, who am I?" she said.

"This is Daisy, the Spirit of Hate," Bill said.

"The time is three o'clock, and this is my time," she said.

"I was about to hear Bill's story; if you can wait, then I can hear yours," I said.

"Wait. Wait! I don't have to. It's my time to speak. You're the one who's behind, not I," she said.

"I need you to wait and be quiet," I said.

"You're too weak to be giving orders. That's why Peter is right here with you. Right now, you're no competition. You're a baby still drinking milk, my love," she said to me.

I looked at Peter, and then he said, "We will hear both stories before we leave, Joe. Daisy will go first and then Bill. We are running out of time. God gives us a place and a time to be for a reason," Peter said.

I was upset, because this thing knew more than I did. After they told their stories, I knew I must read the book Ms. Annabelle gave me so I could get a clear idea of what I was dealing with.

"I'm listening, Daisy. Tell your story," I said to her, and this is what she had to say.

Chapter Six

You Will Never Know

Being filled with all unrighteousness, fornication, wickedness,
covetousness, maliciousness; full of envy, murder, debate,
deceit, malignity; whisperers, backbiters, haters of God, despiteful,
proud, boasters, inventors of evil things, disobedient to parents.

—Romans 1:29–30 (NKJV)

It's been ten years, and they still haven't found the killer. All my work has become cold cases. The clues are right in front of their faces. Not being able to solve murders, do they have the right to call themselves detectives? The victims' families are praying and hoping for the answers to their questions, which are the five Ws: who, what, when, where, and why. Just in case I lost you, let me explain. What happened? When and where did it take place? Who would want to do such a thing? Why would someone want to kill their loved ones? Does the family always get the answers behind these questions? I hate to break it to you, but no, they don't. I know it has to be very painful for the detectives to deliver the bad news. Is there a right way of telling a family that their loved one has been murdered? I don't think so.

Before you begin to judge me, I need to let you know that I do have a heart. I'm not a cold-blooded killer; I do feel for my victims. That's why I tried my best to make it quick and painless, but sometimes, it didn't work out that way. I do allow their bodies to be found right away, so there won't be a need for a search. They are not missing; they're dead. I'm sorry for being blunt with you, but I have to tell it like it is. Am I the only one to blame for the murders? Some may say yes, while others may say no. You know what side I will be on. I should not be the only one held responsible. You are the ones that allowed me to slip through your fingers; yes, it's your fault. The teachers, the therapists, my parents, and the lawyers should be facing time right along with me. Let me break it down for those who have difficulty comprehending. I want to start with my parents; they were the first ones to notice that something wasn't right with me, but they hid it from everyone. When I was five years old, I put the cat inside the microwave. I could hear her screaming and scratching on the glass door, but not once did I have a change of heart. Second, my teachers—some did care while the others were just there to collect a paycheck. If I was a teacher and had a child who always drew pictures of killing someone or something, that would be a red flag for me. Instead, they put me in a special education class, thinking that would solve the problem, but it just made things worse. To me, that seems to be the answer for every school. If they can't get the children to behave, they separate them from the others and put them on medication. That's the wrong answer, if you ask me. Third, let's talk about the therapists; I can't stand it when they don't listen to me. They ask why I am doing the things that I do. When I tell them, they have the nerve to say, "No, that's not the reason." If they already know, why ask me? Sometimes, I feel that they want to experiment on me just to prove that their theory was correct. Finally, the lawyers—I call them the devil in disguise. They all knew that I was guilty, but they fought like hell to get me off, and they did. I always wondered how they could defend me knowing that I'm guilty.

However, it might sound crazy to say that I get excited when I see my handiwork plastered all over the news. There was one particular case that caught my attention. "The body of Henry Jones was found in an alley located between Myrtle and Lewis Avenue early this morning. The police are getting close to an arrest for his murder."

"Such lies!" I would say to myself. To make sure that I was right, I would walk inside the police station just to see if anyone would recognize me. I know this was a stupid thing to do, but I'm a very confident individual. What made them think that they would be able to crack the case if the officers before them couldn't? There are a lot of things that need to be taken into consideration before deciding to become a detective. First, you must be qualified for the job; just because you passed the test to become a detective does not mean you're capable. Second, your state of mind—can your mind process the things you're about to see? Also, one needs to comprehend and devour the information that is given. Third, you must alter your heart, body, and soul. What is meant by that is that in order to catch me, you must become me.

Questions have been asked, and the search has begun, but where would they start? They have no leads, and I've never left any clues. Yes, I do have motives, and each of my victims is linked to each other. That part would be easy to figure out if I operated only in that way, but I don't. It's a must to keep them on the move; twists and turns are also expected. As soon as they think they are getting close, I stop. No need to be greedy; that's when you get caught. Whoever wishes to solve the cases, please do so, but I know one thing: when it's all said and done, you will never have justice. I bought every newspaper and ripped out every article that involves me. The information that's given is incorrect, telling the citizens of Bradford County that they have everything under control when they don't. Sometimes, the news gives out too much information and sometimes not enough. In each case, it could lead to more victims, don't you think?

Bradford Police Department has been working overtime, losing sleep, and barely eating. They have two police officers for every five-block radius to make the people in town feel safe. When they do that, I'm forced to kill again to prove to them that no one is safe, including the police. I wasn't always this way; something happened to me to make me do the things that I've done. I don't think anyone just wakes up and says, "Today, I want to become a killer." For me, it didn't work that way. My life will never be the same; they gave me something that I will always remember, and I must do the same.

Allow me to take you back to my first victim. As I looked around, I saw so many different faces. Some were pleasant to look at, and others had me saying, "What the hell?" with a strange look on my face. Some stared back, while others rolled their eyes. I have come across individuals who have the balls to say, "What are you looking at?" I don't respond, but I do laugh and give a smile. When I do that, I know they think that I'm crazy. I love it when people think that. I hear them whispering, "Stay away, Crazy." Parents pull their kids closer to them as they walk past me. At that reaction, I yell and scream. Boy you should see them run!

Wait a minute; what am I talking about? This has nothing to do with what I wanted to tell you. Give me some time to collect my thoughts; I will be with you shortly.

Where was I? Damn it. I don't know. Okay, let's start here.

As I sat, I heard all the different voices around me—some sweet, some deep, and some in a high-pitched voice that was so annoying. I couldn't take it. "Shut up!" I would say as I turned around.

"Who are you talking to?" she said.

"You," I replied, as I stared at the knife in my hand.

"You know what? I'm not going to say anything else to you!" she yelled and then continued with her conversation. I had to laugh, like she really had a choice. I got up and sat behind them knowing that it would make them move. One by one, they took their time walking by me, hoping that I wouldn't move. I thought hard about messing with them or just letting it go. I chose to let them go, because he walked in. I'd been waiting for him for some time now. My heart was full of hate, and my eyes were full of tears. I watched him walk in my direction. He smiled and laughed with his wife as she held their child in her arms. The baby dropped her pacifier, which I stepped on by mistake. "Oh, I'm sorry," I told them. As we both bent down to pick it up, we locked eyes. I handed him the pacifier hoping that he would notice the scar on my hand. I could tell that he didn't recognize me, and that was a shame. This would have been his last chance to say he was sorry. I always gave my victims the chance to repent for their sins, but they never did until they realized that I was going to kill them. As he stood up and began to walk away, I felt sorry for his wife. She had no idea about her husband's past; because of him, she and the baby would die. I still have the stab marks on my chest, the initials "J.R." written on my right hand and the huge cut in my face that was given to me by her husband Mark Grant. That name I will never forget.

Do you know how it feels to have to look at yourself in the mirror and be reminded of what someone has done to you for the rest of your life? Do you? Answer me, Joe? All because I turned down Mark Grant and his best friend. I wasn't interested in them. I didn't know that rejecting a man would lead to me being hurt and others killed.

On that day, May 17, I lost two important people. Since then, my life had not been the same. I had to take what he loved because he took from me. He had to get back what he had done and more. Nothing was ever even, but it sure made me satisfied. However, I don't blame only him because there were others, six of them. I will find each and every one of them. I must, I have to, and I need to kill them all.

Back to Mark Grant and his wife . . .

I stared at them from the mirror. I watched every movement and read every word they said, even the part where his wife said, "I think we are being watched." He didn't believe her, but she was right. He never listened, even on that horrible night. I was left for dead; if it weren't for that young woman who was jogging noticing me lying there, I wouldn't be alive today. I want to thank her. I owe her my life. The sad thing about it is I don't know who she is. He got up and walked inside the restroom. I stood up, grabbed my belongings, and walked toward the exit. I could tell that she was watching me; as soon as she turned her head, I backtracked and waited in the hallway of the restroom hoping no one other than Mark would come out. I pulled the hammer out of my bag and placed it in my left hand. As soon as he opened the door, I hit him in the face. I could hear the bones crack. He stumbled back and hit the sink. I rushed him and swung but missed. He grabbed ahold of my shirt; I was being swung around like a rag doll. The hammer fell out of my hand during the struggle. I was trying my best to break free. Mark grabbed ahold of my face. My makeup was no longer covering the scar. By the look in his eyes, I knew right then he knew who I was. I began to cry; finally, we were face-to-face. Mr. Grant's guilt made him weak. "It wasn't my idea," he said to me, before he dropped to his knees from the kick I gave to his balls. I picked up the hammer, and he stood up saying, "Please, please, wait." The rage inside took over, and I hit him again, this time in his ribs and again in the back of the head. He lay there bleeding, left for dead like I was. I hurried up and grabbed my things.

* * *

"Joe, someone else is here."

"Where, Daisy? Where?" I said to her.

"Daisy!" a voice called. It was a man standing there in a suit with his dreads pushed back into a ponytail. He also had blisters all over his body.

"Daisy, who is that?" I asked her.

"Oh, that's Mitch," she said to me.

"Why is he here?" I asked.

"Mitch, Joe, wants to know why you're here," she yelled.

"I'm not here to tell my story, but we have a job to do, Daisy. You remember the preacher man Pastor Rice? He's stepping out on his wife again, and tonight, God gave us permission to enter. Satan has called for us," he said.

"I'm sorry, Joe. I have to go, and it works out for the both of us. Now he can tell you his story. We will meet again," Daisy said to me.

"Wait! Before you go, what is your job?" I asked Mitch.

"I'm the Spirit of Disease," he said to me, and they both walked away.

"Peter, maybe we can get to Pastor Rice before they do and talk him out of sleeping with another woman," I said.

"No, that wouldn't be wise of you. God gave that order. Who do you think you are to try to interfere with God's business?" Peter replied.

"I didn't know I was doing something wrong. I'm sorry. Please, forgive me," I said to Peter.

"Joe, it's my turn anyway," Bill said to me.

"Okay, wait; I have to turn the tape over," I said.

"Now I'm ready for you," I said to him.

"It's about time," he said, and then he began to speak.

Chapter Seven

The Killer/You're My Helper

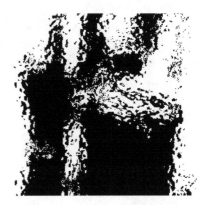

Dearly Beloved, avenge not yourselves,
but leave room for God's wrath, for it is written:
"Vengeance is mine; I will repay," says the Lord.

—Romans 12:19 (NKJV)

Damn it! It's raining cats and dogs outside. I hope I'll be able to make it to my car without getting too wet. As I began to run, everything that I had in my hand fell, including my cell phone. My umbrella flew backward; things were not going well for me right then. I grabbed what I could and started to the car. As soon as I got in, I turned on the car and the windshield wipers. From what I could see, there was a piece of paper tied to it. *Who would do this?* I said to myself. I got out and untied the note. I started to throw it away, but the words that were written on the front of the note caught my attention. The rain caused the ink to run down the page. From what I could make out, the words stated, "I wouldn't throw this away if I were you, Mr. Davis." The wind blew the letter out of my hand. I was in the middle of the street chasing a piece of paper. I caught it before it landed in a puddle of water. I ran back to the car and began to read.

Dear Mr. Davis,

How are you this evening? I hope all is well. As for me, I'm okay. My life could be better, but I'm hanging in there. I know you recognized my writing and my signature stamp so you know who I am. You were the one that testified that it was my handwriting and I was the one that wrote the note that was left at the last crime scene you investigated. You were right, but your testimony wasn't enough to put me away. Yes, I'm free, free as a bird. Now what are you going to do? You will wish you never met me. Who's going to protect you? Not the police, you fat nerd. You can go to them, but we both know that you won't. Do I need to broadcast the truth about Mr. Davis? If you think I'm lying, try me. You are my shadow, and we will work closely together. Now that we are on the same page, I need you to finish reading and do what I ask. Mr. Davis, please believe me, you won't like the outcome if you don't. I just want to tell you my story. Why you? For some reason, I feel we are as one. You might not understand it now, but you will. I always make myself clear. I need you to turn the page because there's more for you to read.

At my trial, Mr. Davis, I sat here listening to both sides pleading their cases. Using words that I couldn't understand, which caused my anger to rise.

I began to stare at everyone in the courtroom; that's the only thing I could do, just for a mental note. Twelve individuals held my life in their hands. You know what I say to that? Bullshit. They're not God, so I hope they know what they're doing. The evidence that they had against me was weak. By the look on their faces, I could tell that they were confused—in other words, it was a deadlock situation. If so, I knew the prosecutor would want a retrial. Her plan was to keep me off the street. They might be able to make everything stick the second time around, but for now, I had to go free. Freedom, that was the wrong decision, but I'll take it. Death has entered the air for the lead prosecutor. I can smell it. Can you? If I was convicted, what would happen to my family? My kids would grow up without a father, and my wife would be left all alone. I bet they never thought about those things. Their only concern was winning. They are cruel human beings. But there's a brighter side behind this madness. Everything I just mentioned doesn't worry me, because I don't have any kids and I killed my wife a long time ago. However, let's not forget about the jury; they have to pay as well. They wanted life for me also. Once again, there wasn't enough evidence to justify the cause. I don't understand why everyone is so angry with me. I've done the world a favor, and look at what I get, you backstabbing, pork-eating fools. Those that I killed needed to die; no one would have missed them. Now I see, even the wicked have to have justice.

Hey, I know you're wondering why I left this note on your car window. I've been watching you for months. I was going to kill you, but the police stopped me just in time, so consider yourself saved. How does it feel to know that you're no longer wanted? To tell you the truth, I'm focused on other things at this time, but if you make me regret my decision, believe me, you will pay for it within every scream. Do I make myself clear, Mr. Davis? I have a heavy load, so I must get started. There's a second note that's lying near the backseat of your car. If you can't find it right away, look again; I know it's there. You need to hurry up because other lives depend on you. Every Wednesday at seven thirty, someone will die. This note needs to be given to Lt. Lewis and only him, no one else. I don't mind; you can read it if you want. Start looking, Mr. Davis.

I began searching for the letter. I had a hard time finding it at first, because my car was a mess. I stuck my hand between the seats and there it was. The second note read:

Dear Lt. Lewis,

I'm so sorry to announce the passing of your wife and your two children. No, don't put the letter down and don't you dare try to call home. Finish reading me, you bastard. I hold you and your partner responsible for not catching my father's killer. Maybe I should say I hold you accountable, because Todd is dead. Now it's just you, and I have to figure out what will happen next. Do you know? Because I don't. I'm getting bored, and when I'm bored, I have no choice but to kill. I told you that we would see each other again. Only in hell, that is what you said to me. I guess you're here with me, because I'm back. You know how hot hell is, so get ready; I'm about to burn shit up.

*   *   *

Bill began to choke.

"What's wrong? Peter, what is happening to him?" I said out loud.

"Stop! No more," a voice said, and then Bill stopped choking.

"Where are you?" I said.

The man with the dog appeared. I moved closer to Peter.

"Don't be scared of him; he feeds off your fear, Joe," Peter said to me.

I moved back, stood like Peter, and waited.

"I'm impressed you made it this far, Joe, but we will see how committed you are to God," he said.

"I have no choice but to stand stronger on God's words no matter what. Even if I cry and have some lonely nights, I can't—I *won't* give up," I said.

"You stupid fool. Do you really think God, your God, cares about you? You're no match for me; you still speak the world's language," he said.

"I know the word of God must be in me. I won't be a baby forever," I said. "And by the way, I know God cares about me."

"If your God cares so much about you, how come he sat there and let your stepfather rape you? He also allowed your brother to be murdered right in front of you, but this is a God that cares?" he taunted.

I stood there with tears coming from my eyes. I remembered Ms. Annabelle telling me that sometimes things happened to you for God to get the glory.

"Nothing to say? Could I be right?" he said.

"No matter what may have happened to me and the things that I have gone through it's because God has a plan for me," I said.

"Really? So what about now?" he asked me, and then James appeared beside him.

"Joe, help me. I'm in so much pain," James said to me.

"James, is that you?" I asked him.

"That is not James," Peter said.

"You shut up," James said.

"Joe, help me like you helped the others," James begged me.

"I can't, James. I can't help you," I said to him, and then his voice changed.

"Fuck you then, you bitch." Then he disappeared.

"Are you done playing here? We have a job to do," Peter said.

"For now, I'm always around, seeking for someone to devour," he said to Peter.

"All of you come with me now," the man with the dog screamed out loud. Unclean sprits came from every direction. There were thousands of them. I knew I would have my day with them all.

"I don't know when I will see you again, but we will catch up with each other, because I have to finish my story," Bill said.

"He's waiting for you, Bill," I said, and they all left.

I fell to my knees and cried, "I can't, Peter; I miss my brother so much."

"God gives us time to mourn, and your time has passed. You have a job to do, and your emotion can't get the best of you, Joe," Peter said.

"It's easy for you to say that; you haven't been through anything but losing material things," I said.

"How sure are you about that statement you just made?" Peter said. "I watched two men rape my sister while the third guy held me down. I couldn't do anything but watch them rape her. After that, they turned around and killed her. At the time, I wanted them to kill me too. Living with those memories, it was too much for me. I was mad at God and the world. All of us have a life story, some worse than others. When you think you have it bad, someone has it worse," Peter said. At that moment, I felt Peter's pain, and seeing him that way didn't make me feel good.

"I'm sorry," I said to him.

"No need to apologize; just be thankful that you're still alive and God is using you for his purpose," Peter said, and then he lifted me up and sat me on the table.

"Sometimes, I feel I won't do a good job," I said.

"Do your best, and God will do the rest, Joe. If you do slip, get back up and try it again. The key to this whole thing is to never give up. You must believe that God is who he says he is and then believe in his words and put them to use. There's no need to know God's words if you don't put them to use. Joe, have faith and trust in God," Peter said.

"I hear you, but—"

"No buts, when there is a but, there is doubt," Peter said.

"It's getting dark, we have to be on our way," I said.

"Are you still willing to go forward?" Peter asked.

"Yes, because I must meet the one and only true and living God who calls himself 'I Am.'" I'm willing to finish; it's too late, and I have come too far. Come, Peter; it's getting dark."

As we began to walk, I could hear footsteps approaching behind us. I quickly turned around to see what was coming our way. "Please wait for me!" a voice called out. A young girl covered with blood was running toward us.

"Joe, I will be right back," Peter said.

"Where are you going?" I asked him.

"You can handle her. It's only blood, Joe. Blood or creatures, which one will you choose?" Peter asked me as he walked away.

"Neither!" I yelled.

"Are you Joe?" she asked me.

"Yes, but I'm in a rush," I said to her.

"That's all right; I don't mind walking with you. I'm so happy that I found you. I know you see those things too," she said.

"I see what?" I said.

"Those things that lie in darkness," she said.

"Who told you that?" I asked her.

"You are the talk of the town; we know your name but are not quite sure of what you look like. There are others like you and I," she said to me.

"Like us? I don't understand," I said to her.

"We see those creatures that wait in the night," she said to me.

"What is your name?" I asked.

"Tina is my name. I'm so happy to meet you," she said.

"I don't know how I'm able to help you," I said.

"Joe, do you think you are only here to help the dead? What about the ones who are still living? Are you going to help us?" she asked me.

"You're the first of the living to come to me. Why are you covered with blood?" I asked.

"Some folks still sacrifice animals for their sins. This blood is animal blood, and to answer your second question, others will come so their stories can be told. You'll meet plenty who are just like you on your journey. We have power. Do you know what your power is?" Tina asked me.

"Power? What kind of power?" I asked.

"Where's the book?" she asked me.

"In a good place," I said to her.

"Good answer, Joe. You have the last copy. Some may even want to kill you for it, but we know not to touch God's anointed ones."

"How many people know I have this book?" I asked.

"Everyone, the good and the evil—both sides want it," she said.

"Why is that?" I asked her.

"You really don't know what you have and how valuable it is," she said.

"I know its worth," I said.

"Do use it; if you did, you would know all your talents your God has given you," Tina said.

"What about you and your talents?" I asked.

"I know what my talents are, but I have chosen to use them for evil," Tina said.

"Why would you want to do that?"

"God's way is the best, but it takes too long."

"But you will miss out on a lot, if you don't do things his way, I hear."

"Is that what you have heard? Joe, what good is it to have the things that God has given and not use them?" she said.

"What are those things, and how do I use them?" I asked.

"Who is with you? Is it Peter Long, Dave, or Lin?" Tina asked.

"I have met all three; have you seen them?" I asked.

"I have met them, but these eyes I can't see from," she said.

"What? You just ran toward us," I said.

"My hearing is not the problem; my eyes are cursed," Tina said.

"If you asked God to forgive you, he would and maybe he would give you your sight back," I said.

"My mouth speaks beautiful words, but my heart holds no truth," Tina said.

"I feel for you," I said.

"Feel for me? Why? We all have the same opportunity of getting to know God. So don't feel sorry for me. Joe, do you know when you are reborn again, the old you dies and you begin to live your life for God?" Tina said to me.

"It sounds like a good thing," I said.

"Yeah, it sounds good, but I can't wait. I want my reward here on earth," she said.

"I was told that you need to have patience," I said.

"Yeah, maybe I should go; I don't want to hold you up," she said.

"I feel that you want to tell me something. What is it?" I asked.

"I know you only take stories from the dead, but I would like to know if you don't mind hearing mine?" Tina asked.

"I can, but I don't have the time to sit and talk with you. What I can do, if you're willing to talk and walk, I will record you and write the things that you spoke about in the book later," I said to Tina.

"I'm willing," Tina said to me.

"Let's get something from the store," I said. "Do you want anything?"

"Yes, but I'm not allowed to go in there," she said.

"What did you do?" I asked her.

"I have some bad habits," she replied.

"You stay here then," I said and walked inside.

I went toward the back and grabbed a few things from off the shelf. I saw Daisy and Mitch standing around. There were so many people in there I wasn't able to tell which one was Pastor Rice. I took my time to see if anyone would say his name.

"Can I help you?" the store clerk asked me.

"No, I'm fine. I don't need any help," I said to him.

"Do you have money to pay for those items or not?" he said.

"Yes, I do have money," I said to him as I placed the items on the counter and pulled out the money.

A man approached the counter and said to the clerk, "Everyone don't want to do you wrong, Bill Ray."

"No, it's not what it looks like, Pastor Rice," he said.

"You need to apologize to this young girl. What is your name, darling?" he asked me as he reached for my hand. As soon as we touched, it felt like electricity left my body and entered his. He pulled away from me and walked back to his seat.

"Here you go, young lady, and please forgive me," the clerk said to me.

I took the bag and walked over to the table were the pastor and this young woman were sitting.

"Yes, may we help you?" she said to me.

I just looked at her and then said to him, "Do you give me permission to speak to you?"

"Yes, of course, speak to me," the pastor said.

"Does your wife know about her?" He began to choke, and then I looked at her.

"Who is she, Phil?" she asked him.

"I don't know," he said to her. He pulled me closer and then said, "How do you know about my wife?"

"Why would you hurt her and your family? You're supposed to be a man of God, and this is what you do?" I said.

"Who are you?" he asked.

"Maybe I should go," she said.

"No, don't leave. I want you to stay, Teresa," he said.

Daisy and Mitch began to get angry. "What is she doing?" Mitch said to Daisy.

"You don't know her and the other men she has slept with, and you're still willing to take that chance?" I said to the pastor.

She stood up and said in a deep voice, "Close the doors."

A plate flew off the wall, split into four pieces, and went into my chest. I fell to the floor. Everyone who was in there was a demon. Each one of them showed his or her true form.

"Jesus!" the pastor called out loud, and then the lights went off.